Jaded by Desire

Lust, Desire, and Love Trilogy (Book 2)

Desiree A. Cox

ISBN-10: 069244453X

ISBN-13: 978-0692444535

Published by Desiree A. Cox

Cover Art: Kellie Dennis at Book Cover by Design
www.bookcoverbydesign.co.uk

Editor: Melissa Gray Editing
www.melissagrayediting.com

Prologue

My mom seemed skeptical when Jeff told her I had passed out because I was dehydrated and hadn't eaten. Maybe it was the look on my face, or perhaps the look on Sky's face, that gave her reason to doubt him. Or maybe it was her feeling of pure disdain toward Jeff that caused her to curl her lips as if she had tasted something foul.

She left the room the same time Sky did, and all I could do was hope Sky wouldn't tell her the truth on the elevator ride down. I knew she would pry.

My thoughts were preoccupied with pastel pink, blue, and yellow baby colors and thoughts, instead of the mint green, light pink, and pale gray colors of the wedding.

I couldn't focus on anything. The Christmas holiday blurred by. Abby had a good Christmas with Sky; that was all that really mattered to me.

I had always been pretty good at keeping secrets, but this one was killing me. It had been about a week since I'd found out the news, and I needed to talk to someone, anyone, but I couldn't. I wasn't supposed to let anyone know until after the wedding. Jeff demanded that.

Jeff wouldn't talk to me about the baby either. He flat out told me on the ride home from the hospital not to talk about it with him. He said he would 'deal with it' when he was forced to. I knew he wasn't happy, but I didn't even know how I should feel about that comment.

I should have been excited with a wedding and a baby on the horizon, but I felt like I wasn't allowed to be.

Mom had returned from her holiday trip. I wanted so badly to tell her, but I knew better. The judgmental comments would roll in like tsunami waves. It would be ten times worse than when I told her about being pregnant with Abby. At least Sky and I were married when I got pregnant with her.

All those years ago, my mom had been concerned because we were young, but she was happy at the thought of being a grandmother. I knew I had Mom and Jim's support, no matter what. Sky's mother had cried at the news that she was going to be a grandmother. She said she thought we were making another huge mistake by having a baby so soon, and she accused me of showing my desperation by trapping her son to stay with me. Sky was outraged and demanded his mom apologize to me. She never did. I didn't let the comment upset me too much. Sky's mom had proven over and over to me that she was unstable and just a bitch.

I didn't even know Jeff's mom. I hadn't met her yet. I had no idea what her reaction would be. Would she be happy? Would she think I did it to trap her son? Who knew.

As I thought back on all the symptoms of my pregnancy with Abby, I couldn't believe I had missed the same signs and symptoms this time around. I guess I just didn't want to think about it.

But things are what they are now. I'm pregnant again and getting married in less than two months.

I trudged through another Saturday morning, my last weekend off before New Year's and before returning to work.

Jeff was supposed to be home on vacation until January second, but the friction between us had gotten so intense that we stopped talking to each other, except for the minimal essential words. When his boss had asked if he was interested in some extra work, Jeff jumped at the opportunity. They had a client in Alabama whom Jeff was asked to go visit for a couple of days and he ran as fast as he could to get away. But now he was due back home later today.

Sky was taking Abby until the next day, like usual. And, like usual, I had to take Abby to him because his car was a piece of crap. I sent him a text.

Me: I'm on my way with Abby

Sky: I'll be here.

Me: Are you alone?

Sky: Yeah. Why?

Me: Just wondered.

After Abby finished her breakfast and I got her cleaned up, we got in the car for the drive to see Sky. My emotions were in turmoil. It might have been the hormones, it might have been the baby situation with Jeff, or maybe a combination of everything. I had never felt so crazy and out of control as I did right then. I wanted to cry half the time, and the other half, I wanted to scream. I just wanted to go back to feeling like my normal self.

I let Abby ring the doorbell; she seemed to enjoy little things like that.

"Hey, baby girl." Sky reached down and scooped Abby up in his arms. My eyes prickled as I fought back tears, tears that were on the brink of revealing my emotional instability. I turned my head, looking back at my car while I tried to regain my composure.

"You coming in, Nik? You know I have a cup of coffee with your name on it."

"Sure," I answered, but my voice cracked. "I could use some coffee this morning."

I stepped in, and Sky closed the door behind me. He set Abby down, and she took off running up the stairs to her room. I followed Sky into the kitchen. The house seemed so much smaller to me now than when I had lived here.

"Have a seat, and I'll get your coffee. You still drink it with sugar and cream, right?"

"Yeah, I …" I sat and stared into the living room, my heart full of despair.

"Nik?" Sky walked over and touched my hand. His fingers were warm. "What's wrong?"

I couldn't speak. My emotions had me choked up. I dropped my head to hide my face as the tears gave away my feelings of hopelessness. I waved my hand, hoping Sky would just leave me alone for a minute. But I had no such luck.

"Damn it, I hate seeing you like this." He knelt down on the floor in front of me, pushed my hair back, and wrapped his arms around me. "I know it's because of him. What did he do now?" He grumbled.

I melted into him and bawled like a baby. He stroked my hair and down my back. "It's okay, Nik," he murmured. He kissed me on the head as his familiar hands comforted me. "It's going to be okay."

"I'm so sorry, Sky. I didn't want to come over here and do this to you."

"Don't apologize to me. I'm always here for you, you know that." He stroked his hands down my face, wiping my tears away. "What's going on? Why are you so upset?" His sincere, caring voice was too much.

I didn't mean to tell him everything, but I did. Through tears and sniffles, I told him that Jeff didn't want kids, that he had gone out of town to get away from me, that he'd told me he didn't even want to talk about the baby, and that he'd *deal with it* when he had to. I told him about the silent treatment I was getting, as if I was being punished because I had gotten pregnant on purpose.

Sky held me tight and rocked me. "It's going to be okay. He just needs time. He needs time to come to grips with all of this. Clearly this all came as a shock to him." He pulled back and held my face in his hands, tipping my head to look up at him. I appreciated his words, but it was a shock to me, too. *I didn't expect this either.* I could see a glint of desire in his gaze, despite the pained look in his eyes. He wiped my tears again, then, without a word, slanted his perfect mouth over my lips, giving me a light, gentle kiss.

I didn't flinch. I extended my neck to meet his mouth and returned the kiss. His next kiss was more passionate, and his tongue found mine. Kissing him was like touching a hot stove; you know better than to touch it because you're going to get burned, but you do it anyway.

He stood and held his hand out to me, and against my better judgment, I placed mine in it. "I'm here for you."

The heat radiated through me as he held my hand. I knew he wanted to comfort me, and I knew what his style of comfort was. I also knew I couldn't let that happen, not again. "This isn't right, Sky. We can't."

"Tell me you don't want this as much as I do and I won't go any further." He looked at me with heat in his eyes. I couldn't lie to myself; I wanted him as much or more than he wanted me. But I couldn't do it.

"I do, that's the problem. But I can't. I'm engaged now, and you have Hope. We can't."

"Why don't we just cut out all the bullshit, Nik? Dump that asshole and come back to me. Hope will get over it and move on. I appreciate and love you, and I'd never treat you like he does." Sky held my hand tighter. "Never." He leaned down and looked me in the eyes. "Don't you think Abby would like to be here with both of us all the time?"

"It's not that easy; and now I'm pregnant, you know," I said. I didn't see us being together long-term. Not anymore.

I would be so mad at myself if I went back to Sky. He was a really good guy, but trying to resurrect a relationship with him would be taking a step back. Yeah, he loved me and wasn't afraid to say it. But I had divorced him for the exact same reason I knew a second chance wouldn't work. I'd always be unsure whether he'd be working in a week.

We both had other people in our lives now, too. Why would I want to ruin what was between him and Hope? And I wasn't going to destroy my relationship with Jeff. I couldn't do it. I wouldn't do it. I loved him.

It would be unfair to everyone. It would be especially unfair to Abby. She'd been through enough. She needed love and stability. We could offer her that without getting back together.

"You know I'd be a better father to his kid than he will." He folded his arms across his chest and stared at me. Sky's demeanor changed -- his entire attitude changed. He seemed upset, but he couldn't really have expected me to say I'd come back.

Once I had regained some semblance of my wits, I continued. "It just won't work between us, Sky. I think, deep down, we both know that. Don't hate me or be mad at me. One day, you'll thank me."

"I don't. I'll love you until the day I die."

I kissed him gently.

Abby ran down the stairs and into the kitchen grabbing my hand. "Mommy, where were you?"

As I looked at her and saw the resemblance between her and Sky, I was so pleased that Sky was her father. I couldn't have asked for a better father for her. "I've been down here, silly. You were up in your room." She was the best of both of us. I ran my hand down her face and smiled, "I love you, Abby."

"I love you too, Mommy."

Abby hopped over to Sky with her arms raised to him. He looked at me passionately as he lifted her into his arms. I could see the love and longing in his eyes. I returned the look because I did still love him, but that didn't change the way things needed to be.

"I have to go," I said.

"Have a nice weekend. Hope and I will have Abby back tomorrow night." Sky gave me a crooked smile. "We're bringing her to you this time, to his house."

Chapter 1

I was so stupid sometimes. I inhaled deeply and sighed out loud. An abundance of regret made my stomach turn. The entire drive home, all I could think about was how close I had been to giving in to Sky, how wrong that would have been, yet how much I had wanted it to happen. *What was I thinking?* I had done the right thing. I did what I should have done a long time ago. I was finally strong enough to say no to him. There wouldn't have been any way to move forward with Jeff if I hadn't said no.

I shouldn't have told Sky about what was going on between Jeff and me, either. That was really dumb. It didn't matter that I needed to talk to someone and he was the only one I could talk to because he already knew I was pregnant. He's the one person I shouldn't be talking to about us, especially not about our problems. *Sky doesn't need to know about any of the squabbles Jeff and I get into.* My mouth just wouldn't stop spilling the details though. If he ever let any of the conversations we've had slip out, Jeff would be so pissed at me.

Another long, exasperated sigh left my lips. I had to learn to just shut my mouth around Sky.

By the time I got home, I saw Jeff's car parked in the driveway. I walked through the door, expecting he might be sitting in the kitchen, but he wasn't. I went to the back window and saw him sitting out by the pool. *Perfect.*

I went upstairs, pulled my hair up into a messy pony-tail on top of my head, slipped on my bikini and wrap, sprayed my body spray on, then went down to face him. We had to talk. Maybe not about the baby, but we had to get our line of communication opened back up. It was driving me crazy that he had gone out of town for a couple of days and we hadn't even texted each other. It was like we didn't even exist to each other for those couple of days.

I slipped through the sliding glass doors quietly so he wouldn't hear me coming. Once I was just inches behind his chair, I bent down and kissed him on the cheek before wrapping my arms around his broad shoulders.

"Come here, you." He pulled me by the hand, leading me around his chair and onto his lap. His hand caressed my face. "God, I missed you, Nikki." His strong hand reached around my neck and pulled me into him, crushing my mouth onto his. Our tongues thrashed with a hunger for each other. He released my mouth and pulled me into his chest, wrapping his arms tight around me.

"I missed you, too. Jeff, I --"

"Let me just hold you, baby doll. I don't want to talk about anything right now. I just need to feel your body against mine."

"All right, we can talk later," I whispered as I settled myself against his chest, my head tilted back just enough so I could kiss against his neck.

His hands stroked my arms, my back, and my hair. "I hated not talking to you. I hated leaving you while being upset." He held me tight on his lap. *You could have at least sent a text. But then again, I could have, too, and I didn't*, I thought.

My nose was buried in his neck, and the smell of his vanilla-scented shampoo mingled with the hotel soap had my senses on overload. I loved his smell. He slid his hand up my back into my hair and pulled me to face him, our lips meeting, again. His fingers skimmed slowly down the front of my neck, down over my collarbone, and made their way under my bikini top where he caressed my hard, waiting nipple. His other hand worked at my nape and the middle of my back to pull the strings that tied my top. He pulled it off and tossed it over his shoulder, exposing my breasts to him. He continued to caress and pinch my nipples. The butterflies in my stomach stirred, and my sex clenched in hopes of his touch there.

"The smell of that stuff you wear is driving me crazy. But you knew that when you put it on."

"I have no idea what you're talking about." I batted my eyelashes innocently.

"Right, pussycat." His hand glided up and down my thigh. He inhaled deeply as we sat in silence for a few more minutes before I spoke up.

"I'm sorry, Jeff."

"What are you apologizing for?" He pulled back from me and stared into my eyes.

"For getting pregnant; I didn't do it on purpose." I swallowed hard. "I swear I never missed a pill. I just wanted you to know that."

"We're not going to talk about it right now."

"We have to eventually."

"Eventually is the key word, but it won't be today." His tone was stern. We sat together for several more minutes.

My stomach growled and broke the lengthy silence.

"Hungry?" His warm breath kissed across my cheek when he spoke.

"I'm starving."

"Let's go to IHOP. I'm pretty hungry, too. Or would you rather go somewhere else?"

"IHOP sounds good to me." I started to get up to go change, but he tightened his embrace on me, holding me in his lap, and assaulted my mouth. Something about his touch, his kiss, seemed different today. There was a strong need conveyed through his attentions, something I hadn't felt before.

When he released me, we went upstairs, got changed, and were out the door in less than fifteen minutes. We didn't talk much on the drive; we mostly just listened to the CD he had in the player. It sounded like some eighties R&B music. I liked it, but had no idea who it was. When it came to R&B, if it wasn't Michael Jackson or the Commodores, I was lost.

I liked listening to the words of songs, and the words in this particular song were thought-provoking. The artist kept saying, *don't disturb this groove; all I need is just me and you.* I couldn't help but wonder if Jeff felt like that. And maybe if he did, then this baby was intruding on our lives, in his opinion. Maybe he thought this baby would somehow ruin things between us. Or maybe I was just reading too much into it.

The next song was a little faster and sounded like it was probably the same group. The words echoed in my head -- you're in my system. Jeff was definitely in my system. I really liked both songs. I had to get my hands on this CD to make sure the DJ had it for our reception.

The songs were a big difference from the Led Zeppelin we had listened to the last time we were in his car. *Whole Lotta Love, Kashmir,* and *All of My Love* replayed in my head for days. He had a vast collection of music.

I stole glances at Jeff's handsome face. He seemed preoccupied. I would have given anything to know what he was thinking right then, but I wasn't about to ask him. He ran his fingers through his hair and seemed like he was deep in thought. He never looked over at me the whole drive, or at least not that I noticed.

We were seated right away once we arrived. The waitress brought us water and gave us the menus. I was immediately hit with the sobering reality that I had to be extra careful what I ate from now on. I couldn't get my normal stack of pancakes, eating as much as I could before I felt like my stomach would burst. I had to eat like a rabbit. I had to make sure I fit in my gown when the wedding day came around. There was no way I wanted anyone to do alterations to it and ruin it. I also didn't have time to drive to Atlanta or anywhere else to find another dress just because I had let myself get too big to fit into my perfect gown. How the hell was I going to manage this over the next couple months?

"Are you guys ready to order?" The waitress held a small pad of paper in one hand. Her face was down as she dug in her apron pocket and pulled out a pen. Once she found it, she never made eye contact, she just put the pen to paper and was ready to write.

"Yes, I'd like the simple-and-fit two-egg breakfast, scrambled egg whites, and wheat toast with the butter on the side, please."

"Anything to drink, hon? Would you like some juice or coffee?"

"I'll have a black coffee and a refill on the water, please." The coffee was going to be horrible black, but I had to eliminate calories from wherever I could.

She turned her head and raised her eyes up from her notepad, and her mouth fell open when her gaze landed on Jeff. She must have missed his gorgeous face when she came by the first time. "And you, sir, what can I get for you?" Her voice became sultrier as she shifted her weight onto her right foot, turned her body toward him, and flipped her flowing red hair. He looked up and smiled at her, which probably made her day.

"I'll have the stack of five pancakes with the butter on the side, and a garden omelet made with egg whites and no cheese."

"No cheese, got it. Can I get you some coffee, orange juice or …" I was waiting for her to finish the sentence and offer herself as a menu item.

"A glass of orange juice and another glass of water would be beautiful." He stretched to see her name tag. "Ann."

Her cheeks became rosy as her smile widened. "Thank you. I'll be right back with your drinks." She collected the menus and walked back to the kitchen.

Jeff reached across the table to my folded hands and held them snug in his. "What else are we going to do today? Any ideas?"

"Whatever you want. I'm open."

"Ah, my favorite position for you."

We were interrupted by our waitress and the tray full of drinks she was delivering. He let go of my left hand, but maintained his hold on my right hand near the syrup containers.

The waitress disappeared and returned in a matter of minutes. Our food was placed before us and he let go of my right hand.

We ate, settled the check, and walked out.

"I want you to meet my mother," Jeff said quickly after we got in the car.

"Great, I'm really looking forward to it." I was excited. I had been wondering when we would meet.

"Today, baby." His voice was full of urgency. "Now."

"Okay."

"But before we get there, I need for you to know some things about her." He wiped his hand across his forehead and then over his chin. "The past six years have been very difficult for her, since my dad passed away. They've been difficult for me, too, but far more so for her."

"Is something going on with your mom?"

"Well, she's ..." Jeff's voice cracked as he spoke. He tried to disguise it with a cough. "I mean, she's better than she was, but she's ..." I watched him swallow hard. I didn't like the feeling I was getting from him. Good news is never this hard to get out.

I reached over and rested my left hand lightly on his arm. He inhaled deeply, then removed his left hand from the steering wheel, reached across his body, and held my hand in his before he released his breath. He sniffed a couple times, not a cry sniff - - just a regular sniff, as he drove in silence for a few more minutes before he began talking again.

❧ Jeff ❧

When we sat in IHOP, I asked Nikki what she wanted to do. I knew I wanted to take her to meet my mom. I *had* to take her.

I hadn't taken anyone to Mom's house since she'd had her stroke. No females, anyway. I wasn't ashamed of her. I loved my mom more than life. But there was no way I wanted to subject my mother to meeting someone who really meant little to nothing to me one week, then when she asks about her, she finds out that woman was out of my life for good.

It was different with Nikki. Nikki was my fiancé, though, and it was time for them to meet.

I made sure Nikki didn't have anything she wanted to do before I sprang my plan on her.

When she replied she was open, my cock jumped. It registered the words before my mouth could reply. She left me in a quandary. Should I take her home and fuck her or go see my mother? I decided going to see Mom was the more important thing to do at that time.

We sat and enjoyed our food, then, after our waitress brought us our check, we got out of there. It was once we reached the car that I got up the nerve to tell her, "I want you to meet my mother."

"Great, I'm really looking forward to it."

"Today, baby." I had butterflies; that super nervous feeling. "Now."

I started the car and the CD jumped to the next song on the playlist. It was one of my favorite groups, Foreigner. My eyebrows scrunched as I listened for a few minutes. I dropped my head and sighed. I ran my hands through my hair while listening to them sing. It all felt surreal at that moment to be in the car with Nikki, my fiancé.

I hoped mom wouldn't be upset that we were dropping by unannounced. I hadn't given her any notice that I was going to bring someone by to meet her. I hadn't even told my mother much about Nikki at all. I had only told her I was dating someone when I got the old 'will you ever settle down and get married' question a month or so ago. I just knew they needed to meet now. I didn't want to wait any longer to do this, and Nikki had already said she didn't have anything else she wanted to do. Plus, I knew the longer I put it off, the more likely they wouldn't meet until the wedding. That would be a total asshole move by me.

"Okay."

"But before we get there, I need for you to know some things about her." I wiped my hand across my forehead and then over my chin. I turned off the radio when the song finished. I couldn't have any distractions or interruptions while we talked. "The past six years have been very difficult for her, since my dad passed away. They've been difficult for me, too, but far more so for her."

"Is something going on with your mom?"

"Well, she's -- I mean, she's better than she was, but she's …"

I took a deep breath and swallowed past the lump in my throat. She reached over and rested her left hand lightly on my arm. After taking in maximum air and releasing, I held her hand in mine. *Fucking shit! This was the reason no one except my male friends had ever gone to see my mom.* I could tell them just enough, and they didn't ask questions.

I was sweating fucking bullets. My heart was jack-hammering in my chest. It felt like it could have broken a few of my ribs. Retelling this story was the worst. The absolute fucking worst. But she had to know. She had a right to know because she was going to be joining our family.

I drove in silence for a few more minutes before I began talking, again.

"Seven years ago, my father had a heart attack." I stopped for a second when I heard her catch her breath.

"It was mild, or so we thought." I paused a few seconds, making sure I could get the words out. "Dad hadn't had any health problems that we knew about before that day. When he was in the emergency room at the hospital, they ran quite a few tests on him."

Breathe, Jeff, breathe. I squeezed her hand gently when I paused for a few seconds before continuing. "They found one of his arteries was ninety-nine percent blocked, so they rushed him up to the cardiac wing and put two stents in to open the passageway. He was put on cholesterol medication and blood thinners immediately."

My emotions had begun to choke me up, all-fucking-ready. "He was supposed to get out of the hospital two days later, but the morning he was going to be discharged --" I stopped. "He …" I choked back my tears and swallowed hard. "He went into cardiac arrest."

I couldn't look at Nikki. I wanted to, but I knew our eyes meeting could do one of two things; either make me shut down completely or fall the fuck apart … completely.

The blood was rushing through my veins, pumping hard. I could feel the pounding in my ears. No one knew what that day or what that whole ordeal had done to me.

No one.

Absolutely no one.

That was the second worst day of my life.

I had been on my way to the hospital with Mom to pick Dad up and bring him home when she got a phone call. I remembered Mom was talking, and then screamed. It was a blood-curdling wail so loud that I swerved the car over to the side of the road, nearly getting us hit. Fucking people were honking and screaming out their window, flipping me the bird. *I guess, looking back on it, I'd deserved it. I had nearly caused an accident, after all.* She scared the hell out of me. I didn't know what was wrong. I had slammed on the brakes, and we sat at the curb. I asked her what was going on. She sobbed so hard and was saying some gibberish I couldn't understand. She finally told me to just drive to the hospital, and that it was Dad. By the time I parked the car, she finally told me what happened.

"They told us it was a good thing Dad was still in the hospital or he wouldn't have survived. He was only fifty-six, and no one expected that, not even his cardiologist. He wasn't overweight or anything like that; he was in pretty good shape for his age." Uttering those words, reliving the events and the fear of losing him on that day made my stomach ache.

I caught Nikki clasping her hand over her mouth when I told her about Dad going into cardiac arrest on the day he was supposed to be discharged. I pulled my hand from hers and began twirling and wringing my wrists. *Jesus, fucking hell. I hated reliving this fucking nightmare.*

"We waited for him to come out of surgery, again, just like the first time. Nothing prepared us to see him like he was as he lay there in recovery. He had tubes and machines hooked up everywhere. His skin was ashen, and his face was expressionless. He didn't even look like my dad; he looked …" The word wouldn't come out of my mouth. I couldn't force it out past what felt like a tennis ball-sized lump in my throat. I could only think the word. *Dead.*

Dad had looked like he was on life support, with a slim chance of survival. I tried so hard to be strong for Mom that day, but I couldn't stop my own tears from falling that day. I had failed her, and failed miserably.

"Every sleepless night we spent in the hospital by Dad's bed for the next week while dad was still in the hospital was spent wondering, and hoping he would wake up the next day."

I was nearing failure at holding it together telling Nikki about this part of my life. It was so hard to swallow. My throat was dry, like I had tried to swallow a handful of sawdust. All of my emotions had collected in my esophagus. My eyes had begun to ache as they filled with tears that I struggled to fight back.

Nikki's soft hands trailed up and down my arm. She made little squeaks, but never said anything. She just listened.

"After Dad got home, he went to cardiac therapy or whatever they called it. He went there for a month and exercised while they monitored his heart. He was supposed to get back to working out at home after that month, doing more cardio, and he did, for the first couple of months." I inhaled deeply. "But I think he got depressed, and just stopped when the doctor wouldn't release him to go back to his job. They told him it was way too stressful."

I sighed, slowly releasing the breath I had inhaled.

I shrugged my shoulders, holding them up tight around my ears, then, after releasing them, I cracked my neck on both sides. My breaths were hard to take in. I could feel my world collapsing around me, again. It felt almost as bad as that day.

"I tried to get him to work out with me, but most days, he said he was just too tired or he would give me some other excuse." I knew I should have pushed my dad and found a way to force him to keep working out. It was partly my fault that he'd stopped. I didn't push him like I should have. *What the fuck was I thinking? I knew he needed to work out. It was my fault. I was every bit as much to blame as he was. It was all my fault.* The more I talked about my dad, the closer I was to falling apart. He was everything to me.

"So, anyway." I coughed. "About two months after his fifty-seventh birthday, not even a year after his first episode, Mom ended up rushing him to the hospital. She told me he began complaining to her about having chest pains." My nosed itched. I scrunched it up and ran my finger just under it hard, then sniffed.

"I don't know the whole story, and I probably never will now, but, Mom said she took him to the emergency room right away." A tear slid down my cheek, but I decided to ignore it. "The doctor who saw my dad said they more than likely didn't come right away like she had told us, but he couldn't say exactly what the timing was without getting more information from my mom."

"What did your mom say?" Nikki scooted over closer to me as another tear trickled down my face. Her closeness soothed me. I could smell that body spray and her raspberry shampoo. It was comforting to have her near me. She was a good listener.

I took the exit off the highway to get over to Mom's.

The next part of the events changed my mood from sad as fuck to mad as fuck. My blood boiled, and I could have sworn I felt steam rise from my collar, burning up my neck when I blurted out, "She said she gave him those fucking pills, those fucking nitroglycerin pills, to make sure it wasn't a heart attack, like the cardiologist instructed. But I don't know why she didn't just call an ambulance as soon as she gave him the first one. That's what she was supposed to do." Nikki pulled back from me slightly.

I sniffed again. "Or she could have called me, for fuck's sake!" I was beyond fucking mad as the words escaped my lips. The tears burned my skin as they rolled down my face. It was like it had been just yesterday. I could have punched a hole through the fucking windshield, but instead, I tapped my hand on the steering wheel, trying not to hit it too hard. I was so enraged, I could have ripped the fucking steering wheel clean off the car. I wanted to scream at the top of my lungs. *Fuck!*

"Do you want me to drive, baby?" I hadn't even realized Nikki had slid over closer to the passenger door, away from me, at that moment. I wanted to let her drive, but what kind of a pussy would I have been? No, I'd drive. We weren't that far away. And I needed her to listen to me, not worry about getting directions to Mom's. I needed to tell her this.

Because this day I was telling her about *was* the worst day of my life.

"No, I'm fine." I wiped the tears from my cheeks, inhaled, and slowly exhaled, hoping to release some of my rage with my breath.

"My mom had decided driving Dad to the hospital made more sense than calling for an ambulance. By the time she pulled in, and they got my dad on a gurney, he had already passed away. They told me his heart failed and his brain had suffered from a lack of oxygen…" I slammed my fist into the door. I was so mad. My dad didn't have to die. He shouldn't be dead. "…at some point before he even arrived." I turned off the engine, and we sat there in Mom's driveway. I gasped for air through my sobs as my body heaved.

My head was throbbing. My body was shaking. Nikki was trying to rub my arm, but I felt like a caged animal. I wanted to get out and run through the woods behind my mom's house. At the same time, I was exhausted from reliving all of this. The anger was trying to resurface as I told Nikki about everything. I just had to be careful not to direct it toward her. I needed her.

"I'm so sorry, Jeff." Nikki scooted back to me and wrapped her arm around my stomach. It felt really good having her there. I reciprocated and wrapped my arm around her back, then pulled her in tighter to me. I could tell by her movements that she was crying with me.

I never wanted her to be sad or upset about anything, including hearing this.

I couldn't stop myself from letting my feelings and thoughts out. They had been bottled up inside of me for six long years, and now, they were spilling out my mouth like that science experiment where you put baking soda and vinegar together in a bottle.

"My dad …" I whispered, then coughed to clear my throat. "Dad was my best friend. I never even got to fucking say goodbye, Nikki. I never got to tell him how much I loved him that one last time." Tears were streaming down my face as if it had just happened yesterday.

Fuck, fuck, fucking shit! I felt like I'd been punched in the gut and jabbed in the jaw a few times.

We sat in silence, and her grip tightened on my arm. She didn't say anything, and I didn't expect her to. What was there to say? And she'd only heard half the story.

"I'm sure he knew how much you loved him, baby." My hands tangled in her hair. I felt so fucked up. Not only was I pouring out my heart about my dad, but she was crying nearly as hard as I was. I hated seeing her cry.

I lifted her head off my chest and turned her face to meet mine. Her mascara was running under her eyes.

And even with that imperfection, her face was the most beautiful thing I'd ever seen. Our tear-filled eyes met.

Jesus, fuck. I loved her. If I wasn't one hundred percent sure before that moment, I knew then, without a shred of doubt, that she was the woman for me. Love was sitting beside me in this car, listening to me. Love was Nikki. I closed my eyes slowly and rested my forehead against hers for a moment before I cupped her beautiful face in my hands and lifted her mouth to meet mine.

I had treated this beautiful woman like shit on more than one occasion just a few short months ago because I had been fighting the feelings I knew were there. I had been a selfish prick, and I felt like I didn't deserve her.

Our lips parted, and I pulled her into my arms. I hadn't even told her about my mom yet.

"My mom, she fell apart after Dad died. She collapsed before we left the hospital. It was a disaster. She was devastated. She had to be medicated for his funeral. Hell, she couldn't even help to get the arrangements made. I had to do all of that."

I left out that Mom had a mini-stroke in the hospital. He was her world, her first love, her only love, her forever love. And she was his.

Watching them together while I was growing up, I knew I'd probably never find that perfect forever love like they had. I didn't think it was even worth trying. I'd heard so many people say a love like theirs doesn't happen often. After desperately hoping with the first few girlfriends and striking out, I gave up trying. Why would I ever think I'd be that lucky?

"We all thought the medication was going to help her get through the funeral and the days that followed."

"Oh, Jeff." Nikki gasped, and another tear slid down her face, following the mascara trail.

"I had to take care of all of Dad's financial business. The months she was in the old house after the funeral were almost unbearable for her. I finally sold their house and bought her this one. It's smaller, and there aren't any memories of her and Dad as a couple here. A couple pictures here and there, but that's it." I loosened my grip on her, then looked into her eyes.

"Baby, she had a stroke right after the funeral. Like, immediately afterward." I was done, a fucking wreck. I gasped and inhaled as the tears fell freely. The tears and feelings that had been stifled for six years broke free. Nikki rested her cheek on my shoulder while she rubbed my back. I could feel her tears soaking through my shirt and moistening my skin.

Not only had I buried my dad that day, but I buried all of my feelings, and had been forced to become my mom's caretaker. "I couldn't be mad at her any longer or blame her for Dad not getting medical attention sooner," I choked out past the lump, tears flowing freely.

I couldn't grieve that I'd never see my dad again. I couldn't grieve that my mom would never be the same again. On that day, I was forced to bury all of my feelings about all of this at that very moment. I had to do it because that was what my mom needed me to do. I couldn't lose them both. I inhaled and sniffed as I worked to pulled myself together.

"While Mom was in the hospital, I found out that my dad had heart disease, and it was hereditary. His father, my grandfather, had the same disease, and he had died when he was forty-six. I guess my dad had talked to the cardiologist about his family history, and the cardiologist told me. I didn't even know until that day. I wasn't completely against having kids, but when I got that news, I knew I never wanted any kids of my own. How could I do that to a child? And why would I want to pass something so fucked up on to them? It was bad enough I had to live knowing that it was part of my genetic make-up." My blurred gaze was shifted down to her stomach knowing that baby; that innocent baby, could have this passed on to them and it would be all my fault.

I had to get a fucking grip. I was sitting there, crying like a fucking little child. I wiped my face. "After Mom was released, I spent a lot of time here with her, feeding her, taking care of her. I finally had to have a nurse come in when I started traveling for my job. I still come see her every week, usually Friday or early Saturday before I come home, after I get back in town." I dropped my head, and I saw a tear fall onto my leg.

She rubbed her hands down my face and looked at my teary eyes. "Baby, I'm so sorry." She leaned in and kissed my cheek. "I wish I could have met your father. I'm sure he was a wonderful man, and I know I would have loved him. But, right now, I really do want to meet your mother."

Nikki was wonderful. As broken up as she was, she was my strength. How could I have tried to run her off? I was a monster. I didn't deserve her.

"Mom doesn't get around the best now, and her speech is still slurred. You have to be patient with her, Nikki."

"She's your mom, Jeff. I'll love her like she is my own." I felt like I was in a fairy tale, and Nikki was my un-fucking-believable perfect princess.

I got out of the car and walked around to help her out. As I stood outside the passenger door, I noticed she seemed to have a bout of lightheadedness and lost her balance. I closed the distance between us to make sure she didn't fall. She looked like she was on the verge of passing out, then, after a couple minutes, stood up straight on her own and sighed.

I had to feel her; I needed her in my arms. I wrapped my arms tight around her waist and crushed my lips on hers, inhaling her spirit into me, then pressed her back against the car. I felt a deeper connection to her now, and I didn't want to let her go.

I couldn't let her go.

Ever.

I had to protect her with my life.

When I released my mouth from hers, I took her hand in mine, and then we walked up to the door and rang the bell.

So many nights I had cried alone while submerged in the thoughts of my father. I had been bottling this up for a long time. I was finally with *my* special someone whom I could share all of this with.

Chapter 2

I was so mentally and physically exhausted when we returned home that I had to go lie down. Jeff came up and joined me. It had been a long day. His naked body wrapped around mine as we lay there as one. His hand stroked my outer thigh and back as his warm breath caressed my neck. Before long he was snoring and his body had stilled. *My poor baby.* I had never seen a man so torn up with emotion the way he was as he had recounted that day for me.

I laid still beside him. I listened to him snore, and my mind couldn't let go of the conversation during the drive and visit to his mom's house. My heart was still aching for him. I wanted so badly to take all of his pain away. Watching him fall apart and shatter before me had left my heart in tiny fragments.

Yet as broken as he was in the car, he was ten times as strong once we walked inside his mother's house. He had a wide smile on his face as he embraced her. She was so happy to see him; the love between them was undeniable and tremendous. He introduced us, and she gave me a look, her mouth twisted and her head bobbed, as she took me in from head to toe, then back up again. I wanted to laugh, but knew that would be very rude; instead, I just smiled at her. I saw in his mom, Lisa, the shell of a beautiful woman who had once been very physically striking.

She told us to come in the kitchen, so we followed her. She walked with some difficulty, as Jeff had warned me. Her left foot dragged, and she looked like she had a limp. After we moved into the kitchen, I realized she couldn't use her left arm; it hung limp at her side. She also had slurred speech, struggling occasionally to pronounce certain words, and her face on her left side seemed to have much weaker muscles than her right side. Through the entire visit, Jeff was super patient; he never tried to finish a sentence for her and held her hand in his nearly the entire time we were there.

The nurse, Karen, treated his mom like she was her own mother. She made sure she had water since her mouth dried quickly. She was cooking dinner, which smelled fantastic. She didn't leave his mom's side, but wasn't overbearing either.

When Jeff told his mom we were engaged and were getting married, his mom turned to me and her eyes became slits while she stared at me. Without any warning she had asked me, "Are you pregnant?"

I glanced at Jeff and saw him subtly shake his head, and I replied, "No."

Throughout our conversation, she had asked me four more times if I was pregnant. Each time, I told her no. I felt so terrible lying to his mom. Somehow, I got the feeling she could tell I was pregnant. I don't know how she knew, but I felt like she did.

When we got in the car to come home, I had to turn my head away from Jeff. The song on the radio was too much, on top of everything that had happened.

I woke to Jeff's soft lips pressing against my neck and arm with light kisses.

"So long, baby," he whispered. "This feels so right being with you. I've been waiting for you to come into my life."

I arched my back to rub across him. I felt his erection pressing into me. A flood of want washed over me, and the familiar tingling sensation surfaced. I rolled to face him, wrapping my arms around his neck. I ran my fingers through his hair and pulled his mouth onto mine. Our naked bodies molded together perfectly.

The words he said had that song replaying in my head.

He pulled my leg up over his hip and rubbed his tip against my slit, sliding slowly down to my opening. He slipped his crown inside me and moaned deep in his throat while he bit my bottom lip, then took control of my mouth. His taste made me curl into him.

"Mmmm." He sank deep in me. "Damn, baby," I mumbled.

His hand stroked through my hair, and he pulled my mouth into his. He demolished my senses. His smells made me crazy. I could smell his clean hair, his not-so-perfectly-fresh breath, his skin. His smell was that flawless heady, savory-musk that was uniquely him. He claimed me; his tongue swiped across my lips and tongue. His taste was salty and sweet; he tasted so good, better than any piece of candy I had ever eaten. His look was smoldering. His eyes were heated and full of desire.

His skin was soft and smooth, stretching over his rock-hard muscular chest and abs. I wanted to dig my fingernails in and climb up him, like climbing Mount St. Jeff.

And his moaning and ragged breathing was going to be my undoing. I couldn't get enough of him. He had me hook, line, and sinker. I wanted to scream.

He pressed deep into me, rocking his hips in and out as we remained on our sides. "You feel so fucking good, Nikki." His words unhinged me as I clenched around his thickness, pulsing and exploding as he continued to stroke me.

"Damn it!" I grabbed a handful of his hair, my stomach muscles contracted, and my hips thrust forward to feel every bit of him pummel my core. "Jeff!" I pulled myself up his body, pressing into him, and surrendered myself to him. "Oh, fuck me!" I screamed.

He rolled me onto my back, grasped my legs behind my knees, pressing my legs up toward my head, and continued to thrust into me. "Damn, girl."

Damn was right. I couldn't get enough. I grabbed his ass and pulled him into me tight. I wanted to help him fill me.

His strokes were long and slow. He wasn't fucking me; he was making love to me. He needed my love. I needed his love. A tear slid down my temple at his gentle approach and the memory of the words from that song. My hips rocked to match his rhythm, meeting him as he sank deep in me. I selfishly wanted him to go faster, but, at the same time, loved that he wasn't in a rush. I loved him with all of my heart and never wanted to let him go.

I never wanted this moment to end.

Never.

His hands reached under my hips, lifting me to him for a few more strokes. He rested my feet on his shoulders before his hands made their way up to stroke down my cheeks. "Look at me, baby doll." He was staring deep into my soul, touching my heart. I was his; I was so lost in him. He slid my legs off his body, then bent and kissed my lips as his strokes intensified. "You're so beautiful, baby. I –" He stopped his sentence as I came undone beneath him.

"Oh … Oh." I unraveled. "Jeff … shit!"

He hammered into me over and over. "Fuck, baby doll." He fisted a handful of my hair as our bodies collided. His hand pinned me by my hair, pulling it, but I didn't care. He could have ripped out chunks of hair right at that time and I wouldn't have cared. He slammed into me with so much force that he was moving me across the sheets, and my head was hanging off the side of the bed. I knew he was close.

I saw stars as we found our release together, and I felt his seed fill me while my sex convulsed around him.

"God … damn it!" he screamed. He collapsed down on top of me, and I could feel him pulsing inside me. I was more than happy to take his weight on me.

He rolled to my side, and we lay there moaning, wheezing as we tried to catch our breath. The day could end right now and I'd be happy to just lie here, sated, snuggled up to him. I was floating high above cloud nine.

"Are you all right?" His hand caressed down my cheek, under my chin, and down across my collarbone.

Oh god, I'm more than all right. "Jesus Christ, Jeff, I …"

"I know, baby, I know." He kissed my lips. "I fucking know."

We had connected on a higher level. Earlier, he had shared his emotions, really deep emotions. Did that mean he loved me, too? Even though the words never came out of his mouth, I knew he did. That day, I could feel it. I had never felt such a strong emotional connection, and he had never made love to me before; we had always fucked. Oh, the fucking was good – great! – but this was amazing. A smile spread across my face, and my heart felt like the rays of sun were streaming directly into it. Yeah, he loved me.

Jeff raised his head. "Pussycat, it's almost seven o'clock. What do you say we go down to the movie theater and watch a movie? I just want to sit there with you in my arms."

"Sure, why not? We need to get something to eat, though, baby; you made me work up an appetite."

"Trust me when I tell you, food is the number two priority on the list, behind taking a shower." He slapped me on my ass. "Let's go."

Chapter 3

My mind raced as fast as my heart was beating. One more month until the wedding, and I was going out of my freaking mind. Checklists, planning, loose ends, packing for the honeymoon, and work -- it was all taking a toll on me. Hiding being pregnant aggravated the hell out of me, too. So many times, I almost slipped.

I couldn't shake the feeling that I was lying to everyone by not telling them. Yeah, yeah, I was withholding information, so it wasn't the same, right? As soon as that thought would go through my mind, I called bullshit on myself. I didn't even believe myself when I thought that.

I especially hated keeping the news that I was pregnant from my mom. That was the worst. Jeff had lied to her, flat out. I hoped when we finally told her that she didn't get mad and that she would understand why we kept it hushed, but the likelihood of that was slim. It wasn't like keeping it from Jackie, Mandy, or Georgia; this was my mom. I was expecting her to blow a fuse when it all eventually came out.

My first doctor's visit was coming up in a week. Mom had gone with me and Sky for the first visit when I was pregnant with Abby. This time, I'd be going by myself. Jeff wasn't even going with me. My only consolation was that the first visit wasn't a terribly big deal. Conveniently for him, he was going to be out of town. I couldn't help but wonder when he was going to accept the fact that we were having a baby; that he was going to have to admit to himself that he was going to be a father. I sat at my computer, shaking my head.

"You look like you have a lot on your mind." Robert, a co-worker and my replacement while I was going to be out of the office, startled me out of my daydream.

"Oh, yeah, just a couple things."

"Do you mind if I ask you a few questions? Is this a good time?"

"No, I don't mind; pull up a chair." Since we worked in the same area, Robert was going to be picking up some extra accounts while I was out with the wedding and on my honeymoon.

"So, I was looking over a couple of your accounts to see how you were making updates, and I glanced over the report. I noticed a couple things that didn't seem right so I dug a little deeper and saw some numbers had been transposed." The hair on the back of my neck rose. That was exactly what Jack, my manager, had hollered at me for a few months back. "I made the corrections to those accounts, but the report is off now. By a lot."

I took in a deep breath. "Thanks for pointing that out to me. I can fix the reports."

"If you don't mind, I'd like to sit with you so I can see how you do that. Just in case I need to do it while you're out." At the rate I was going, I should have planned to begin my leave right after I showed Robert how to make the adjustments.

We sat together for the next couple of hours. We walked through some of my other accounts to make sure there were no other errors there, which there weren't. Then I showed Robert how to make the adjustments so the report was correct. It wasn't as easy as making an update on a screen; he had to go into the database and make the change there. It was a lot more risky to have to make database changes. Once all the changes were made, we ran the report again, and *voila,* perfect.

Robert thanked me for going over that with him. I was able to answer some other questions he had, also. Soon after he left, Georgia came by to see if I was interested in going across the street to get pizza. I was always up for food. I felt like I was starving all the time. Even after I ate a meal, I was still hungry. The problem was, I couldn't eat much. I was completely paranoid about gaining even an ounce. I had to make sure that dress fit me in four weeks.

Candace and Georgia met me out by the elevator. "Are you getting excited?" Georgia asked. "Only one more month before the big day."

"I am; I can't wait."

"I know it's going to be beautiful. I'm excited, too," Candace chimed in. "Is Jeff getting nervous?" We stepped out of the elevator and made our way across the lobby.

"I don't think he is, or at least, he never shows it. He always seems so cool and calm. I'm a frantic mess, especially when he's home. I feel like I'm nagging and making sure he's getting things done, but it doesn't seem to faze him much."

"I've been talking to Jackie about your bachelorette party in the coming weeks. First, let me say, I love her." Georgia flashed a wide grin. "We were thinking an all-male revue is in order."

I pressed the crosswalk button. "I don't know about that. I don't want to be put on stage or have some strange guy grinding all over me like that in public. I think I'd rather have something maybe a little more low-key."

"You can't be selfish; you have to think about the rest of us, too." Candace laughed.

"I'm not telling you guys what to do. You're planning the party; you don't need me to help with this. I'm just giving my two cents since it was brought up. Please, don't take me anywhere in public and have me groped and dry humped into humiliation."

"The only promise I'll make is no public dry humping." Georgia opened the door to the pizzeria and we all entered.

"That's all I ask." We ordered our pizza and made our way to the cashier to pay for our food before we found the least crumb-covered table with three chairs. "Jeez, I guess it's too much to ask for a clean table. That would be nice."

"Relax, Sparky," Candace said. She pulled out a couple of napkins and wiped the table off. "There you go."

"Thanks. I didn't mean for you to clean the table."

"I know, but they are pretty busy, especially around this time of day."

"Yeah, I guess. I'm on edge."

"You do need to relax. Hey, I don't think you ever told us what the doctor said about your lightheadedness." Georgia took a bite of her pizza as she looked at me. She swallowed. "It really sounds like blood pressure to me."

"My appointment is next week. I'm curious what they think it is, too. They didn't find anything when they ran all the tests in the emergency room. I can't imagine they'll find anything now." I already knew what it was, but I had to keep pretending. *I was scaring myself with the ease of telling all of the lies*, I thought. "It's probably nothing, just nerves and anxiety, with everything going on right now."

"Probably; you do have a lot on your plate," Georgia added.

"Yep, after the honeymoon, things will get back to normal for you and you'll be feeling good as new." Candace smiled at me.

I only ate half of my slice of pizza before we gathered all of our trash to toss out. I was starving. It hurt like a bitch to roll up that half a slice of pizza into the napkins and plate, then throw it in the trash. *Fucking hell.* I felt like I was going to pass out from lack of food. I knew I wasn't starving, starving, but, man, my appetite had seriously increased.

We made our way back up to our department, and I waved at them both as they walked back to their desks. I sat at my desk and fantasized about food for the rest of the afternoon.

Chapter 4

I hadn't realized how fast two weeks could pass. The hours and days seemed to be on fast-forward.

I also would have never guessed in a million years that I'd find myself at a party to celebrate *my* upcoming wedding where I couldn't drink. I was with all my friends who did drink, and all I could do was watch them. That made it seem like it was going to be one of the hardest events of my life, and definitely the most difficult celebration for me to get through. I knew the questions about why I wasn't drinking with them wouldn't stop until the night ended.

Jackie and I had arrived at Georgia's house an hour early to help make sure everything was set up and ready for the party. Well, Jacking was anyway.

I had told them I preferred not to go out, which went against everyone else's wishes. Since Jackie and Georgia were planning the party, we were going out. They unanimously wanted to go to an all-male revue show, then head over to Sunova Beach to finish the night with some dancing and more drinking, something else I had expected. I couldn't drink, though, and that really sucked.

When Georgia opened the door, she was already a couple drinks in. I couldn't blame her. It was a party, and we had hired a limousine service for the night so no one had to drive. Since Georgia lived alone, most everyone had planned to stay, at her house when we got back, just in case they had drank too much to drive. I wasn't going to stay, and neither was Candace. Candace didn't normally drink much, and she wanted to get home to her husband. I wasn't drinking at all, so I would be more than capable of driving home. I was more than willing to go home and sleep in my own bed, next to Jeff's warm body.

Georgia welcomed us in and was quick to pour two glasses of wine, one for Jackie and one for me. In an effort to not draw too much attention to the fact that I couldn't drink, I accepted the glass and made up my mind I was going to pretend to drink that one glass all night. *A couple drops surely wouldn't hurt me or my secret bundle.*

We chipped in and helped set out the snacks and the drinks for mixers on the dining room table. Georgia's kitchen counter looked like a full bar, complete with every type of liquor anyone could ever want. You name it, she had it. She also had many different red and white wines.

Her kitchen and dining room were creatively decorated in the penis theme for the party. She had penis straws, penis stirs, penis whistles, and penis-shaped ice cubes. She had set out the cake shaped like a penis on the dining room table in between two penis-shaped candles, and there was a small bowl of penis mints near each candle. The mints were delicious. I chuckled to myself at the thought that quickly raced into my head: *of course they're good, I love penis*. She had a long banner of several penises taped up above her sink in the kitchen and another hanging in the dining room. It all made sense knowing we were headed to a male strip show later. I smiled and shook my head.

We had invited ten women in total for the bachelorette soiree. My mom had declined, but offered to pick up Abby Sunday morning from Sky's place, then she'd come to the rehearsal and deliver her back to me. Another friend from college had declined, so we were expected to be a party of eight for the night.

As the time got closer to seven o'clock, one by one, everyone showed up.

"Are you still on that first glass of wine? You need to drink up, girlfriend; we've got one hell of a night planned for you," Jackie said.

"I'm pacing myself. I don't want to get drunk too fast."

"That's smart," Georgia added. "Too bad I didn't think of that about two hours ago."

We all laughed.

Jackie and Georgia made sure everyone was introduced before we played the first game -- pin the dick on the stud.

After everyone had a drink in their hand, Georgia briefed all of us on how the game was to be played. "So, ladies, here's how this works. Each of you gets a paper dick from my lovely assistant, Jackie." The whoops and whistling began. "You're going to be blindfolded, get spun around twice, pointed at the wall, and you will pin your game piece on the poster. The one who gets the closest to correct anatomy placement will win a prize."

"What's the prize?" Candace said and laughed.

"That's a surprise, but - you'll love it. Well, if the winner doesn't, someone here will." Georgia was so funny. I had only seen her teetering on being intoxicated one other time. "Jackie, please give them their dick."

Jackie handed each lady a paper dick with a push pin stuck through the head. "Everyone gets to feel a Prince Albert piercing gone wrong."

"I'm passing a pen around; write your name on your piece so we know who gets the closest. To help with figuring out who goes first, I have everyone's name in this bag, and I'll pull them out one at a time, then you'll take your turn." Georgia shook the plastic Publix shopping bag, then reached in and pulled out a slip of paper. "Caitlin, you're first."

Caitlin was a friend from college and one of the dorm resident assistants. She was always nice, and we had stayed in touch over the years. She had been at my first wedding, which made me feel kind of weird when I prepared to send her the invite to wedding number two.

She set her drink on the end table and stepped up near Georgia to get the game kicked off.

Jackie tied the blindfold on her then tested to make sure she couldn't see. She was spun twice, turned to face the huge unic poster-boy, and told to go. She wobbled a little as she made her way to the wall. She felt for the edges to make sure she at least stuck the poster, attached the penis, and stepped back before removing the blindfold. Laughter erupted. She had placed it on his arm. That gave a little more advantage for the next person. Caitlin headed for the kitchen and began mixing up another drink.

Georgia stuck her hand in the bag and pulled out the next name. "Candace, you're up." Candace finished off her drink before setting her glass down.

"I'm ready; blindfold me," she said. Jackie quickly covered her eyes and tied the straps behind her head, performed the two-second vision test, and began spinning her.

Once Candace was pointed toward the wall, Jackie turned to me. "You aren't done with that wine, yet? What's taking so long? Hurry up so I can get you a refill."

"I'm fine, don't rush me. I don't want to get too drunk tonight."

"The way you're going, Grandma, you won't get a buzz at all." Everyone laughed and I returned a smile to them. There was no way I was going to be so irresponsible to drink myself stupid just to make them happy. Even if Jeff didn't want to acknowledge it yet, I had his baby in my belly and preferred for him or her not to come out of me needing to be checked into an alcohol rehabilitation clinic.

The game seemed to drag on, and eventually, it was my turn. I was the last person. I had sipped about half of the wine by the time I was told to come up and faced Jackie. "Drink that wine all gone before I tie this on you."

"I can't, my stomach is bothering me. If I drink too fast, I might get sick."

Connie, my old neighbor, and now Sky's neighbor, jumped into the conversation and asked, "Are you pregnant?" I tried not to let it be obvious when I rolled my eyes. *What in the actual fuck? Is that shit flashing on my forehead?*

My face flushed. "No, I drank too much last night with Jeff. I just don't have a taste for anything alcoholic tonight. But we're still going to have fun. I don't have to get wasted." Surely that would buy some leeway for me on the drinking.

"Whatever, put the glass down, bitch, and turn around." Jackie seemed annoyed, but knowing her, she really wasn't. She just enjoyed calling me a bitch. I set my glass down and let her tie the blindfold on. She spun me around, and, as many uneventful times that I'd been spun in the past, this time made me feel dizzy and a little queasy. I swallowed hard a couple times before getting a push in the back to get walking. I felt around, holding my arms out straight, and just stuck my piece on the wall.

Everyone laughed and cackled. I stepped back and removed my mask. *Oh-my-god!*

"Everyone, meet dickhead," Gloria said. She laughed hysterically, with everyone else joining in, including me. Leave it to me to be the one to put my piece *above* Caitlin's, right on the poor man's head.

"Okay, so the winner is Connie. She got the closest to right. Here's your prize, my darling." Georgia handed her a wrapped box. "Oh, and you have to open it here."

Connie ripped the paper off and gasped. "Oh my! I have a new boyfriend." She held up her gift, a rabbit vibrator. I never had understood that thing.

Jackie stepped forward and spoke. "Congratulations, Connie, hope you enjoy that. We're going to have Nikki open her gifts, then we have another game to play."

Everyone screamed and hollered as if they were at a concert. Most were visibly on their way to being quite intoxicated. I, unfortunately, was not.

I was escorted to a chair in the living room, and all the gifts were brought in to me. I opened seven gifts and was the recipient of seven different pieces of very sexy lingerie, most in black, one in red and another in white. There were a few two-piece items and a couple that were only one piece. One of them had attached garters and thigh-high stockings. Jeff was going to love these women. I planned to pack each one of the items. I had a couple new items stashed in my collection that would round out the trip, and would surprise him in something new each night we were in Hawaii.

"Thank you all so much," I said. "Thank you for coming, and thank you for these wonderful gifts. I'm sure Jeff thanks you too; he just doesn't know it yet." We all laughed.

"You all ready to keep the party going?" Jackie pulled a paper bag out from behind a lamp. "For the next game, we're playing charades. Everyone knows how to play, right?" Everyone was nodding their heads and some replied yes. "I'll pass the bag around, and you pick what you're expected to act out. Georgia will be picking names from her bag for the order again. We have to go kind of fast because the limo will be here in about a half hour. And I'm going last."

She walked around and made sure everyone got their slip of paper from the bag.

Georgia, who was working on polishing off her next drink, threw all the names back in her plastic bag, gave it a shake, and pulled the first name. *Lucky me, I was up first.* She pulled the coffee table back out of the way, opening the space between the seating in her living room. I moved to the center of the room as they all circled around me, sitting on the couch, loveseat, and chair.

I inhaled deeply. *Here goes nothing.* I took a minute to gather my nerve to make a complete ass of myself. I bent and got on my hands and knees, and the suggestions started.

"Submissive."

"Animal."

"Doggy-style."

I began crawling around, feeling more awkward than ever. This might be more fun if I was two sheets to the wind, but sober, it was just humiliating. I began licking my tongue around my lips, then thrashed it in and out of my mouth.

"What in the hell?" Jackie laughed.

"A toad."

I crouched down a little lower and continued to stick my tongue in and out.

"A snake."

I felt like I had been down on the ground for an eternity. *Jeez, someone guess this shit right already.*

"A lizard," Caitlin finally said.

"Yep, a lizard." I stood and smiled. *Thank God someone guessed it.*

Everyone else had taken their turn except Jackie when the doorbell rang. Thirty minutes had already passed, and she didn't even get to do hers. I know she was a party organizer, but it didn't seem fair to me. She held up her slip of paper then said, "I'm going to need help." She went and opened the door, and the chauffeur was standing on the porch. She invited him in as she assured him we would be ready shortly. I went to the restroom, a side effect of the surprise package in my belly, and heard the music start up.

When I walked out, I saw everyone sitting in the living room having another drink. "Are we going out or what?"

Georgia answered, "Yeah, we're going. We'll leave in a few minutes, when this song is over or we finish our drinks, whichever comes first."

I sat in the chair that was across from the fireplace. A new song was started, and I saw, out of the corner of my eye, our chauffeur removing his jacket and stalking toward me. *Holy shit, he's a stripper.*

He had a perfectly sculpted, muscular form that, if I hadn't been so used to Jeff's fantastic body, would make me drooled. He stood right in front of me. He flipped his hat off, over toward the couch. He ripped his pants off, tossing them the other direction to the loveseat. Then, he stood there in that piece of barely-there, just-covering-his-junk loin cloth and proceeded to give me a lap dance. I'd never had a lap dance before, but was very appreciative of his fine talent. He was able to swivel his hips, grind and rub against my thighs, all while balancing and holding himself up with his powerful, flexed thighs. He made his chest muscles jump for me, then held onto the arms of the chair as he snaked his body up mine over and over. I knew it was wrong, but I was really enjoying this man's performance.

When the music stopped, he gave me a hug and a peck on the cheek, before wishing me well and conveying his hope that I'd have a long and happy marriage. He told me my fiancé was a lucky man, which made me blush, and I thanked him. He had an incredibly deep, and sexy, voice.

He really was our driver, too, and was there to take us to Whiskey North. The club was putting on a Saturday night show. He redressed himself and said he was ready when we were. Being sober and watching those crazy friends of mine gave me a glimpse of what I looked like when I drank. It wasn't like seeing them made me want to give up drinking. I was looking forward to drinking in five months, but I wouldn't drink to excess again. Not on purpose anyway.

We got to Whiskey North, and the pressure to drink started up again. Jackie went to the bar and bought shots of Fireball for all of us. I pressed my lips together and rubbed my forehead. *How was I going to get out of this?*

"On the count of three, we slam these. Here's to you, Nikki. Be happy." Jackie offered up the toast. Everyone added in their sentiments as we did the celebratory glass touching thing. I wasn't sure exactly how I was going to pull this off, but I was getting ready to *not* drink this shot.

As everyone tipped up their glass, I turned and tipped mine halfway, and bumped my arm into a woman who happened to be passing by us. I dropped my glass on the floor for good measure. Fortunately for me, it didn't break on impact.

"Oh my god, I'm so sorry," the woman said.

"It's okay. I shouldn't have turned."

"No, I should have been looking. I was trying to get back to our table and wasn't even paying attention. Let me buy you another drink."

"That's okay, really. I didn't need it anyway."

"No, I insist."

"Fine, if you insist, I'd like a glass of Moscato, please."

"Done, I'll be right back." She bent down, picked up the glass, and walked to the bar.

"What the hell, man?" Jackie said. Her mouth was scrunched in a scowl, and her eyes were shooting daggers.

"Don't worry about it; she's getting me another drink."

"No, it's a sign. You didn't do your shot with us. That's fucked up. You know that's bad luck."

"Oh, shut up, don't say that."

"Seriously; you were supposed to drink that with us and you'd have had good luck going into the marriage."

"Well, we can toast again when she brings my fresh drink."

"We can, but there are no do-overs."

I was feeling a bit taken aback by Jackie's explanation of my impending bad fortune, knowing she already didn't like Jeff, and that she was now talking this bad luck bullshit. The woman returned with my wine. I asked her if she had ever heard of the old wives' tale that Jackie had told me about, and she said she had, and had friends who experienced the bad luck -- they were divorced now. With a fifty percent divorce rate, it didn't surprise me. Don't blame it on some ridiculous superstition; maybe they just weren't meant to be together.

The woman suggested we all do another round of shots and make sure I drink my drink this time. Jackie summoned the waitress nearby, asking for another round for us all, except me, at my insistence. When she returned, in an effort to stave off any negativity, I hoped that one sip of this wine wouldn't hurt my little seed. There was no way I was going to chug that entire glass. I held my lips to the glass and made it seem as though I was downing my wine after the round of toasting and clinking took place. Our new friend hugged me and darted off to rejoin her party.

We sat in the VIP seating, and had the best seats in the house. There wasn't a bad location in the club. If I had to classify it into three sections, I'd say good, better, and best. We had a great time. I was able to forgo getting on stage, instead letting Georgia take my place. One lap dance was enough for me, and by the way it looked, Georgia loved being up there in my place. We had so much fun, we never did make it to Sunova Beach.

When the night was over, our driver took us back to Georgia's house, where everyone, except Candace and I, stayed. It had been a long night, and I was looking forward to crawling into my own bed and getting some sleep.

When I got home, I noticed Jeff had not made it back yet. He had his bachelor party that night as well, and I didn't expect to see him until we woke up in the morning. A quick flash of insecurity meandered through my mind while I was getting some ice water. *What if he doesn't show up until the morning? What if he's out living it up with someone else or up to his eyeballs in strippers throwing themselves at him? What if he changes his mind about marrying me?* I brushed all of those silly thoughts aside, dismissing them as last-minute jitters, and proceeded up the stairs. I stripped naked and crawled under the sheet.

I was awakened when I felt Jeff's weight behind me and felt him snuggle his chest up close against my back. His arm draped around my waist, and I felt his glorious, naked skin against mine. I didn't smell any liquor scent. He hadn't been drinking.

It wasn't long before and I was roused out of my sleep unexpectedly. Groggy and half asleep, Jeff had slid his hand down to my crotch and was rubbing me. My response to him, even waking out of my sleep, was immediate and full of desire. He turned my face until my mouth was met by his crushing mine. My body turned until I was lying flat on my back. The sex was hard and intense. There was no foreplay, just instant, hot, hard, nocturnal sex. It was amazing. When we both found our release, he pulled me flush against him, and we laid there together and drifted into dreamland.

Chapter 5

The alarm went off at nine in the morning and startled me, but not near as much as waking up alone in the bed. When I had reached over to Jeff's side, I felt the cool sheets. He had been up for a while. I was hoping I could have awakened nestled in his strong, muscular arms.

I dragged myself from beneath the sheets and headed in for my shower. We had a long day today. Jeff had an appointment to get his hair cut, and I had to make sure all payments had been made. Then we both needed to start packing for our honeymoon. And we had the rehearsal and rehearsal dinner later in the afternoon. Running through the to-do list in my mind told me something wasn't going to get done.

As I exited the shower, I smelled food being cooked. *No way*, I thought. *He's cooking breakfast?* I quickly slipped on my clothes and ran down the steps into the kitchen. I made it just in time to see Jeff plating up food for two.

"Good morning, beautiful. I was going to surprise you."

"You already have. You surprised me first by being out of the bed before me, and, second, by cooking." Our meal wasn't elaborate, but it was special because he had made it for us. We had scrambled egg whites, toast, and microwaveable sausage. It was the thought that counted, and I was starving.

"I had to get up and get moving. My appointment is at ten thirty so I have ..." he looked at the clock on the stove, "about a half an hour to eat and get out of this house."

"This looks delicious, thank you." I loved him so much. As imperfect as he was, he was perfect for me. I leaned in and gave him a kiss after he sat down at the breakfast bar, then took a seat next to him. "We only have one more week, Mr. Carrington, then we'll be married."

"I know. Are you feeling like running away? Maybe being my run-a-way bride?" He nudged my arm with his elbow as he scooped some egg whites onto his fork.

"Not a chance in hell. I'm not going anywhere." I leaned in towards him and bumped his shoulder with mine.

"Good, saves me from having to gather my posse to come hunt you down." We both laughed. We sat and ate our breakfast, then he kissed my forehead before running upstairs to finish getting ready.

By the time he came back downstairs, I was finishing cleaning up the dishes. "I'll see you later, babe. I'm going to get Connor and Sandy. I probably won't be back for a couple hours."

"That's fine, just remember, we need to be at the Rusty Pelican no later than four this afternoon for rehearsal, then dinner afterward."

"I won't forget."

"If you want to just meet me there, let me know."

"I'll call and keep you posted. See you later." He leaned in and kissed me, pulling me into him tight. He took my breath away.

He released me, grabbed his keys off the counter, and headed for the front door.

"I love you," I called behind him.

"Back at you," he replied. He pulled the door tight behind him.

I went in to the conservatory and pulled all of the wedding invoices out of the desk and began sifting through them to find the ones that weren't already marked as paid. I couldn't help but think that having an office would be really nice right about now. Jeff had left me a credit card to make sure everything was paid for, so I called and paid the five remaining bills.

I went upstairs to pull together my dress I planned to wear at the reception after the garter was tossed, and some comfortable shoes so I'd be able to shed the four-inch heels I was going to wear with my wedding gown. I didn't have any of my wedding things here at the house; all of that was stored at Georgia's. I was making sure nosy Jeff didn't get a peek of my gown before I walked down the aisle on our wedding day. While I was in the closet, I pulled out my suitcase, tossed it on the bed, and opened it, then began tossing in things I knew I wanted to take to Hawaii.

We were going to be there for ten days, ten whole days. I was so excited to be away from work and away from everything for that long of time. The hardest part of being away was going to be missing my little munchkin, Abby.

My attention was drawn to the airline tickets on top of the dresser. We would be spending three nights on the Big Island, three nights in Kauai, and three nights in Maui. I grabbed the tickets off the top of the dresser and zipped them in the outside zipper pocket of the carry-on bag I was planning to bring to make sure we didn't forget them.

I sat on the edge of the bed, then fell backwards onto it. I couldn't believe how my life had changed in such a short period of time. Less than a year ago, I was single, living in a small house, living paycheck to paycheck, and struggling to make ends meet. Today, I was living in a huge house with no more money concerns, getting married to a wonderful man, the love of my life, and he was the father of my unborn child.

I couldn't wait to share the news about the baby with everyone after we got back from our honeymoon. I envisioned my mom being happy with the news, instead of being upset that we had kept it a secret from her.

A lot had changed with Sky over the past few weeks, too. I still loved him, and I knew I always would, but I was no longer holding onto the life we once had. I loved him dearly as the father of Abby, but I wasn't *in* love with him anymore. I was able to move on. And, what was even better, he had moved on, too. He and Hope -- yes, fucking gorgeous Hope – reconciled, and Sky admitted to me he thought he was falling in love with her. I was so happy for him, for them. All I ever wanted was for him to be happy. I had gotten over my jealousy of her. I actually liked her a lot. She was a wonderful person and loved Abby almost as much as we did. She was moving in with Sky in two months. I couldn't ask for anyone better to be a part of all of our lives.

I held my hand up and stared at the ring on my finger. I was living a dream life.

I laid there with my eyes closed, basking in my happiness, when I was startled back to reality by my phone ringing. I glanced at it before answering.

"Hey, Jeff."

"Hey, baby. You don't mind if I meet you at the Rusty Pelican, do you?"

"Not at all; I was expecting it."

"Cool, we are going to hit the mall real quick. Connor needs to stop in the Tux shop."

"No problem, just please, tell him not to make you late. If you're late, I'll be upset. I don't want to start this rehearsal late."

"Wouldn't think of upsetting you; we'll be there. I'll see you later."

"Bye."

I rifled through my drawer and pulled out all of my new lingerie I was gifted at the bachelorette party and packed them in the suitcase, then pulled a nice silk pajama set out to lay over them all so Jeff wouldn't see them. That pajama set was his least favorite thing to see me in. I laughed to myself.

I found a couple of swimsuits and tossed them in the bag. I looked up and saw it was almost two thirty; time was flying by. I zipped my bags up and pushed them back against the wall. I'd have to keep working on the packing during the week.

I stood in the closet, flipping through my clothes to find something nice to change into. I found a flower-print, mini-sundress to slip on and my white jewel-top sandals. After getting changed, I went downstairs, made sure the back door was locked, grabbed my purse and keys, and headed to the Rusty Pelican. I sent a text to Jeff before I left the driveway, letting him know I was on my way.

By the time I pulled into the parking lot and found a parking spot, I saw Jeff and his mad shopping crew pull in. I stood on the sidewalk at the edge of the lot and waited for them. Connor jumped out of the car and ran over to me, wrapped me in his arms, and swung me around.

"You're going to make me sick, Connor."

"I'm so happy for you both, Nikki. I knew it when we first met you, that you were the right one for this big lug."

"I can honestly say, I didn't think I was, but I'm so happy you slipped me his card." He set my feet back on the ground just as Sandy and Jeff walked up.

"Hey, you got a hug for me, Nikki?" Sandy asked.

"Of course, sweetie." We embraced, and then he released me.

"You look more beautiful every time I see you."

"Thank you." I could feel the heat flush through my face.

"All right, stop mauling my woman," Jeff joked. He wrapped his arms around me, pulled me in tight, and planted one hell of a kiss on me. He held my head to him by my hair. *Damn, I loved when he did that.*

"Jeez, get a room already," Connor said.

We all laughed, then made our way up the ramp to the entrance. We were a little early, but when we stepped inside, we saw Georgia and Candace were sitting there, waiting.

We all exchanged pleasantries, and I introduced everyone. Georgia's eyes sparkled during the introduction to Connor. Hunter, one of Jeff's good friends and occasional work-out partner, and Jorge walked up, with Mandy close behind them. Hunter was breathtaking, as always. I had to be extra careful not to stare at him in front of Jeff, but I let him sweep me up in a hug. I did another round of introductions, finishing just before my mom and Jim arrived with our little flower girl. Abby had a big smile on her face and a small basket on her arm. When they walked in, I let Jeff introduce everyone. I looked at my watch. "It's four o'clock on the dot; Jackie should be here …" I looked up and saw her walking up the ramp to the door. "Now."

We introduced her to everyone she hadn't met before, and then the hostess took us all back to the Grand ballroom. Jeff stayed in front waiting for the officiant to arrive. It was only a couple of minutes before they both joined us in the ballroom. The wedding planner for the Rusty Pelican was there as well and helped walk us through the plans for the wedding day. After an hour and a half of practicing the ceremony and going over the reception details through the first dance, the hostess came back to let us know our table was ready whenever we were.

We decided to be very informal with seating for dinner. We didn't think we needed to tell adults where they should sit. We had a seat for everyone, and they would certainly all figure something out. Mom and Jim sat down near Jeff and me. Abby sat on my lap. The waitress tried to get her to sit in a booster seat, but she didn't want anything to do with it. She bounced between my lap, Jeff, Jim, and Mom. Our orders were taken, and the waitress disappeared. She returned a few minutes later with our drinks.

I noticed Georgia had sat down next to Connor, which didn't surprise me. I actually had expected that. Jackie was sitting next to Sandy and across from Hunter. It was good to see everyone talking and getting along.

We gave everyone two entrée choices: Herb-seared salmon or Filet Mignon. I didn't have either, I chose the Lobster and Mango salad. I thought it was a good choice and it didn't have a lot of fat or calories.

Before our food arrived, Connor and Jackie ordered champagne for everyone so they could offer up a pre-wedding toast. I knew not to drink mine; instead I pretended by putting the glass to my lips and making it look as if I were drinking. I received a bump to my leg under the table and a stern look from Jeff right after the toast, after he lowered his glass. *Was he coming to grips with reality?* I glanced at him over my shoulder and gave his leg a gentle, reassuring squeeze. Shortly after the toast, our servers brought out our food.

"Darling, you're barely eating anything. Are you feeling well?" Mom asked after watching me pick around in the salad.

"Yes, I feel fine, just not terribly hungry." The truth was, I was starving, but was scared to death I was going to gain weight and not fit in that beautiful dress.

"Make sure you eat, dear; you don't want to get sick, not now."

"Don't worry, I'll make sure she gets plenty of rest and eats," Jeff said. Mom smiled at him with her thanks-for-your-comment-but-I-wasn't-talking-to-you glance she had perfected over the years as she patted my hand.

We had a great meal. We wrapped up our dinner by eight fifteen, and I was completely exhausted. Mom and Jim left early. I thanked them for coming and for everything they had done. They helped me out so much with Abby, and especially over the past weekend. The officiant left right behind them.

We all finished and exited the restaurant just after nine. Abby had fallen asleep on my shoulder shortly after Mom and

Jim left, so I carried her out. I hated that I had to drive myself home. All I wanted to do was go home and lie down.

Jeff and I thanked everyone for coming out and for being part of our wedding party. We gave them all their gifts that night to make sure we didn't forget on our wedding day.

"Babe, you and Abby ride home with me. We can come get your car tomorrow."

He didn't have to tell me twice.

Chapter 6

The days between the rehearsal dinner and wedding went by so quickly. I was supposed to have been off all week, but instead was asked to work on Monday and Tuesday because Robert had a family emergency. But when he returned on Wednesday, the work week ended for me.

Jeff was home all week. As large as his house was, we seemed to be in each other's way quite a bit. We spent the rest of the week finishing packing. We also had to make sure we had our things to take to the hotel and to have on our wedding day.

I had to pack Abby's things, too. Sky only had a few changes of clothes at his house for her. I made sure any last minute loose ends were tied up. I called in the final head count to the planner at the Rusty Pelican so she could make sure the kitchen had that information and answered a couple questions for her.

On Friday morning, I dropped Abby off at day care and took her bag over to Mom's before going to my hair appointment. Sky was going to pick Abby up and go by Mom's to get her things.

I wasn't completely sure what I was thinking when I scheduled an appointment at eight thirty in the morning. I was so tired, I fell asleep in the chair while getting my hair blow-dried. They woke me when it was my turn to move to the styling chair. My hairstyle for the wedding was going to be elegant and simple. I wanted loose curls that were swept over to one side and pulled up off my shoulders, but into a soft-looped ponytail, or something like that. I had decided against any type of head piece; instead, I had a decorative hair comb with faux pearls on it. Simple. Jeff wanted to have real pearls sewn on it for me, which was incredibly generous of him, but I was afraid I might lose it and told him no.

By the time I returned back home, Jeff had already left to go to Connor's. He was going over to make sure he had everything ready to take to the hotel.

I was going over my list, doing the same. Neither of us was looking forward to sleeping in a hotel or apart, but we decided, that we would not break tradition. We'd stay there the night before and night of the wedding. The morning after the wedding, we'd come home and get ready to go to the airport.

Being at the hotel, we weren't so far away that we couldn't come back by the house if we needed to because we forgot something. Jeff and the guys had a suite they'd stay in, and my bridal party and I would be doing the same on the Wedding Eve. The night after the wedding, Jeff and I would be in a suite of our own, and they all could stay in those rooms together, again, without us.

Jackie was on her way over to help me get everything that wasn't already at Georgia's apartment, to the hotel.

My nerves were doing a number on me. I hadn't eaten. My stomach felt completely empty, hollowed. My chest was tight, and my nerves were causing tingles to run through my thighs, weakening my legs. I was hungry, but didn't feel like I could eat, not now, not and keep it down. The anxiety and excitement going into the weekend was bowling me over. In less than twenty-six hours, I would be Mrs. Jeffrey Carrington. The doorbell snapped my fantasizing. I ran down the stairs and flung open the door.

"Hey, Jackie."

"I was expecting a butler, but I guess you'll do." She chuckled. "This place is fucking nice as hell." Jackie stepped into the foyer and began looking around. "This is the second or third time being here, and I am still in awe." She stepped into the living room, then back to the foyer before looking up the stairs that led to the balcony.

"So, are you ready for this?" Jackie sang out. Her voice was all it took to turn me into a tearful mess. My words wouldn't come out; my emotions surrounding this weekend had an invisible grip on my throat. All the crying and tears were annoying the hell out of me, too. *Damn the hormones!* I thought I had things under control, then it just took that one small thing, that one simple question, to prove me wrong.

She came closer to me and pulled me into her embrace. "Don't cry." She stroked down my back. "You're still planning to get married, right?" All I could do was nod my head into her shoulder.

"Bitch, you better. I spent too much money on that dress, shoes, jewelry, and my hair." I couldn't help but laugh. Leave it to her to find a way to chip away at my emotional funk and brighten my mood. God, I loved her so much. I loved everyone right now. I even loved strangers in the damn grocery store.

"I -- I'm okay," I stammered. "I'm sorry; everything seems to make me cry lately."

"Don't apologize to me. It's cool. I get it." We walked back to the kitchen.

"It's so irritating, though. I feel like such a crybaby. My emotions are in stupid overdrive right now. I cry over the dumbest shit."

"I'll make sure to have extra tissues tomorrow, just in case. But just remember." Jackie waved her finger in the air at me. "If you get too out of control with your crying tomorrow, your make-up will run, you'll ruin your pictures that you'll have to look at for the rest of your life, and you'll look like hell in front of all the guests." We both laughed.

"And that, would be very fucked up," I quipped as I wiped the last bit of moisture from around my eyes. "Do you want anything to drink before we get started?"

"Nah, I'll get something when we get to the hotel. I have a few bottles of wine in the car for later."

"I meant a glass of water." I laughed and shook my head. "I'm not going to drink tonight. I'm just letting you know now. Even the slightest weight gain and that dress won't fit."

"Fine, more for me." We both laughed, and I nodded my head in the direction of the stairs. "Before we go up, show me around."

I had forgotten, Jackie had never seen the entire house before. She had come to pick me up a couple times, but hadn't gotten a walk-through. I walked her around, showing her the first floor before we went upstairs. After giving her a quick peek in each of the spare bedrooms, we went into Jeff's bedroom. I skipped the basement. I'd save that for another time.

"This place is really nice, Nikki." Jackie kept looking around, opening the closet doors and glancing in the bathroom.

"Yeah, it is. Jeff's house sure as hell beats that house I was in."

"Wait a minute, why did you just call this place *Jeff's house*?"

"Because it is. I moved into his house. My name isn't on it."

"Yeah, but you live here. Don't you put this address on all of your mail?"

"Of course I do."

"Then it's your house too, right?"

"Yeah, I guess it is."

"So when you marry him tomorrow, whose house will it be? Still just his?"

"All right, it's our house. Is that better?"

"Don't try to convince me; you need to convince yourself."

"Come on, we're squabbling over nothing. We have to get this stuff into the car so we can get it to the hotel. I still have to make sure Georgia gets everything out of her house, too."

We grabbed bags and boxes of items that I had sitting in a hallway to be taken to the hotel. My make-up, my shoes, regular clothes to lounge around in, and toiletries. I also had to take my second dress for the reception. I couldn't believe how much stuff I had. Jackie couldn't either and told me I looked like I was moving out. *Maybe we should have just gotten married in the backyard; it would have been easier.* We finally got everything in her car just before Jeff came back home.

"Hi, Jackie." His tone was aloof, but he was trying to be nice.

"Hey," she replied.

"You guys are going to take good care of my girl tonight, right?"

"Absolutely. We're going to get her drunk, then hit the strip club. We'll probably keep her out all night."

"That wasn't quite what I meant." His lips thinned, and he glared in my direction.

"We aren't doing that. I just felt like yanking your chain."

Jeff walked over to me and snaked his arms around my waist, then bent his head to whisper in my ear. "I'm going to come steal you away later, just for a little bit. I can't stand that I'll be away from you all night." He pressed his cheek against my head and inhaled deeply, then lowered his lips onto mine. His kiss was gentle. It stirred my stomach and heated me between my legs. He lifted his mouth from mine enough to whisper, "I need to feel you wrapped around me tonight." He held a handful of hair in each hand and pulled me close to him. "I intend to make you scream later, pussycat." I gasped as he took my mouth again.

"Are you two done?" Jackie was tapping her toe, staring at us with that save-it-for-later look on her face.

"I'll be waiting for you, just text or call." My panties were soaked at his promise. We didn't have our own room, so I wasn't sure of the logistics, but I knew Jeff would figure something out. I gave him another quick kiss, told him bye, and left with Jackie.

We had decided to go by Georgia's house before going to the hotel. We could get my wedding gown and shoes in the car, then Georgia could meet us at the room when she was ready.

To our surprise, when we arrived at her house, she had everything in her car and was ready to leave. She followed us to the hotel. Once we turned into the hotel driveway and parked under the overhang, we scrambled to get a cart and loaded everything on it to take to our room.

"Wow," Georgia exclaimed. "This is it. Tomorrow's your big day. How do you feel?"

"Nervous and excited."

"You'll be okay," Candace interjected. "It will be over before you know it. Then you'll be happily married and in Hawaii." We were all surprised to hear her voice. We didn't expect her to arrive until later in the afternoon.

"Make sure you take pictures in Hawaii. Lots and lots of pictures. I may not make it to Hawaii ever in my life, but at least I can see it through your pictures," Jackie stated.

"Trust me, pictures will be the last thing on my mind while I'm there." My eyebrows danced up and down before I gave her a quick wink.

"Bitch, take pictures. You have to come up for air at some point."

"I will, I promise. I was kidding. We have some activities planned to get us out of the room. I plan to take a ton of pictures."

"Do you think you guys will have kids? I mean, I don't mean to pry, but I'm just curious," Georgia asked with a sheepish grin on her face.

"I don't know, maybe. We haven't really talked about it."
It wasn't completely a lie. Yes, we were having at least one, but
we hadn't talked about it, it just happened.

"You'll probably come back from your honeymoon
pregnant. You hear those stories all the time." Jackie was
touching on a very sensitive subject. She had no idea how right
she was. She hit the nail smack-dab on the head. I'd be coming
back pregnant all right, but only because I was pregnant before
we even left.

"Um, yeah, maybe we can talk about something else.
Like where the hell is Mandy?"

"Oh, she called me; she's not going to get here until
around seven tonight." Candace and Mandy seemed to hit it off
quite well when they were introduced. It didn't surprise me she
had called her and let her know she would be running late.
Mandy had to have known I was going to be a freaking mess
today.

"Well, let's go get checked in. I'm ready to go up to the
room. We can text Mandy the room number so she can just come
straight up when she gets here."

I stepped up to the front desk, got us checked in, and we
walked down the hall and around the corner to catch the elevator
up to our room. Once we got in the room, I sent a text to Jeff
letting him know we were here and what room we were in.

We made quick work of getting everything hung up in the closets to make sure we didn't end up having to iron our clothes. The last thing we needed was that to slow us down tomorrow.

Jeff

I couldn't believe tomorrow we'd be married. I never thought or expected we'd actually still be together to make it to this day, honestly. I went from not sure I wanted to talk to her, then after meeting up with her, thinking I didn't want to be anywhere near her. Now, I wasn't able to stand being away from her. I was so caught up in her. Pussy-whipped is the exact way Hunter describes me. That's cool, I'll be that. I'll tattoo that label on me. I just can't live without her.

I was going to hate sleeping in that hotel, alone. I needed to feel her body next to mine. I loved feeling her soft skin pressed close into me.

If you ask me, that whole 'don't see each other before the wedding' was some bullshit made up back in the day when women were virgins and couples didn't fuck or live together before they got married. What does it matter these days? If my cock was buried in her last night, why couldn't it be tonight, too? Why couldn't we sleep in the same bed? Is it just me? *Bad luck my ass -- I'm calling shenanigans.*

Well, fuck that superstitious crap, I had every intention of stealing her away from her friends tonight so I could feel her writhe beneath me. My cock jumped at the thought. Even that head knows Nikki should be in my bed with me.

Just as Connor and I were leaving his house to get our tuxes and all the other stuff into the hotel, I got a text from Nikki letting me know they had checked in. She sent the room number, but with Jackie, the pit bull there, I doubted very much that I'd stop by. I didn't want to have to deal with her trying to enforce the whole you-aren't-supposed-to-be-together crap. I was happy that Jackie and I were able to get along most of the time, though. That was progress.

After we got settled in, it didn't take long for Hunter, Sandy, and Jorge to arrive. We ordered room service. They sat around drinking Fireball shots, but I passed. I had plans. I had to drive later. At the rate they were going, the only one that would probably realize I even left would be Sandy.

Hunter was apparently still drowning his sorrows over that worthless ex-girlfriend of his. She was ridiculously hot, but her fucking personality was as flat as a dull rock. How he spent an entire year with her is beyond me. She was fuck-and-duck material only.

After another couple hours of talking, I had had enough. My friends were great, but I needed to see Nikki. I pulled out my phone and sent her a text.

Me: Can you sneak out?

Nikki: Give me about ten minutes

Me: Meet me downstairs in the lobby

Nikki: OK

I felt like a teenager sneaking around behind my parents back.

Chapter 7

I woke before everyone else with my stomach in knots. I had a feeling deep in my stomach that something had been overlooked, something didn't get finished. Some detail had not gotten the proper attention. I knew it was technically too late to do anything about it, but I wished I could put my finger on what was gnawing at my nerves.

I sent a text to Jeff. We knew we shouldn't see each other until the wedding, but that didn't mean we couldn't chat.

Last night had been amazing. I liked spending time with my friends, but I loved spending time with Jeff. We made a trip back to the house. There's nothing like being in your own bed. Then reluctantly returned to the hotel where we said our good-byes and returned to our respective rooms. I had to agree with Jeff, that tradition of not sleeping together seemed way outdated.

I rose and made the bed, then began pacing. I had to try to figure out what was causing this concern, what was driving me insane. I pulled out my laptop to review my planning document. My brain was turning to lumpy gravy, and I had to rely on notes for damn near everything. I scanned up through all the tasks on the plan and noticed I had confirmed everything except the music and DJ, but it didn't seem like that was it, that I felt so unsettled over music. I knew Jackie and Connor were more than capable of getting that taken care of. There had to be something else.

As I scrolled up the page, there it was, under the list of tasks to do one month before the wedding. I hit my head with the palm of my hand. *I fucking forgot to write my wedding vows.* During the rehearsal, we never actually said them; we just told the justice of the peace we were going to write them ourselves. And I forgot. *Fuck!*

I picked up the hotel notepad near the phone and began scribbling words just when someone knocked on the door. I glanced at the clock, then slipped on my silk robe before walking over, and peering through the peephole. Mom was standing on the other side of the door. I quickly unlocked it and let her in.

"Good morning, Mom. You look beautiful."

"Good morning, sweetie. How are you? Are you ready for your big day?"

"Ugh," I moaned. "I forgot to write my wedding vows. I can't believe it. Of all things to forget, not that."

"You don't need to write anything and prepare a canned speech. If you love him, you can just talk from your heart."

"I *do* love him, Mom, there's no *if* about it," I snapped, and my annoyance at her comment was evident.

"I know you do, dear, I didn't mean to say it like that. I was merely making the point that you don't need to prepare anything in writing."

"You're right, I don't. But what if there's something I really want to say and I don't say it?"

"You'll have the rest of your lives together to tell him how much you love him and tell him anything else you forgot today."

A tear streamed down my cheek. We had the rest of our lives together to tell each other how much we love each other.

"Sweetie," Mom started, "I think you need to pull it together. You can't cry through this entire day."

"I'm trying, it's just that this —" I stopped myself and looked off to a corner of the room, hoping my surprise at my near slip wasn't obvious in my facial expression. It was killing me not to tell her. But in two more weeks, I could tell her and the world.

"It's just what, Nikki? What are you keeping from me?"

I couldn't believe I had almost let it slip that I was pregnant. "It's just that I've never loved anyone as much as I love Jeff. I love him more than I loved Sky."

"It's a different type of love. With Sky, I could tell you loved him very much, but it was that young, first love. The kind that is pure and innocent. The kind you hope will last. With Jeff, your eyes twinkle at the mention of his name, so I know he has won your heart. It's a more mature type of love, the kind that can last forever, if you work at it and you want it to." Mom pulled me into a hug. I needed to hear her reassurance. And even though she would never admit it, her comments were a way of admitting she was accepting Jeff as my husband.

"I think you need to start getting ready. You should make sure the dress you plan to change into during the reception is kept out so you can hang it in the room. Then you can grab it quickly when you decide to change. Make sure not to forget the shoes." Mom released me from her arms.

We continued our chatting while getting all of my things set up and lined up. One by one, everyone else woke up and joined us in the living room area. I had slept on the pull-out sofa, but had made it and folded it back up already. I thought that was the easiest and less disruptive of arrangements since I was only going to be there one night.

As everyone else gathered in the living room, I pulled out my phone and saw I had a text from Jeff. I was lost in the thought of him as I sent a reply 'good morning' text back to him.

"Are you texting with Jeff?" Candace asked me.

"Yes." I blushed.

"Good grief. No wonder you didn't hear us. We are going to make a food run. Do you have a preference?"

I looked at the clock and noticed it wasn't even ten o'clock yet. "I'm fine with an Egg McMuffin from McDonald's, no cheese or meat. Just something light for me. I don't want to eat too much." I returned my attention to texting.

"Um, what's going on with you, Nikki? You've been eating like a bird lately," Georgia asked.

"Just making sure my dress fits perfectly, that's all." I kept texting as I walked over to my purse, pulled out my wallet, and then handed my credit card to Jackie.

"You don't think they'll ask for ID?"

"Are you kidding me? No."

I told them to make sure everyone ordered what they wanted and to get me a black coffee. Jackie and Georgia were going to make the trip to get our breakfast. Mandy and Candace were going to help me get our things gathered.

Mom was a lifesaver. That was typical for her. She made sure we all kept working to get ready since we really had hoped to leave the hotel room by One o'clock pm. We had a limo coming to get us so we didn't get delayed by the shuttle that would be transporting our out-of-town guests.

After we finished eating, I was ready to begin getting dressed. I pulled a pair of cut-off shorts and a tank top out of my suitcase and slipped on my flip-flops. They all looked at me like I had sprouted a second head. "What? Why are you guys looking at me like that?"

"Those hillbilly shorts and that tank top. Really?" Jackie wrinkled her nose in disapproval.

"I'm changing when we get there, remember? I'm not getting married in this. Plus, I need something that can fit in my purse."

"We have a bag for you, but it's whatever. It's just for the ride," Candace chimed in.

"Hopefully you don't freeze, it's not ninety degrees outside." Mandy said. She made the call to the front desk to make sure the limo was notified to come pick us up.

While we waited, Jackie touched up my hair, making sure it was perfect. She grabbed my make-up bag for me and made sure it was in the duffle Candace was holding. Georgia carried my dress I was going to change into and the shoes.

We double checked and made sure we had everything we'd need, then headed down to the lobby. It was only a few minutes before the limo arrived to pick us up and take us over to the Rusty Pelican. I was a tightly-wound nerve ball. Everyone else was laughing and having a good time, while I sat quietly in the back seat.

Once we arrived, the driver helped us get everything inside. It didn't take long before I heard the music begin to play.

Jackie and Connor had worked on the playlist to be used while the guests were entering for the wedding ceremony. They had done a fantastic job. I didn't know half of the songs playing, but I loved them all.

I looked at my watch and knew it was time. I hung my gown on the hook of what appeared to be a storage closet door, and we began the process of getting me ready. I shed the shorts and tank before slipping on my dress. I was ecstatic that it fit perfectly, exactly like when I tried it on. And there was no visible sign of a baby bump. My stomach was still as flat as it had been when I tried it on the very first time. When I was four months pregnant with Abby, I had already been in maternity clothes.

Jackie, again, touched up my make-up and hair, and this time, she gave me a pretty heavy coating of hair spray. She slid the faux-pearl comb in along the ponytail holder. There wasn't a lot of talking by me, but they all kept chattering away. I handed Jackie the pearl necklace I was going to wear so she could fasten it for me. Once she finished, I replaced my stud earrings with the beautiful dangling ones I had chosen.

"You're mighty quiet, Nikki," Mom said as she sat in a chair, watching all of us.

"Yeah." That was it. That was all I could think to say.

We were all working hard to get me ready so we didn't start the wedding late. I had been to a few before where the wedding start time on the invitation was stated, but the wedding actually began a half hour to an hour late. It was so fucking annoying, and I wasn't about to do that to my guests.

The music changed, and I looked at my watch. Two thirty, only thirty more minutes before I'd be standing face-to-face with Jeff. My heart skipped a beat.

The planner came in the room. "How are you all doing? Are you almost ready?"

My mom spoke up for us. "We will be. Right, honey?"

"Um, yes. We will be. How much longer?"

"We should begin lining up in about fifteen minutes. I'll stop back in. I'm going to go check on the guys real quick." She eased the door closed behind her.

"Are you getting nervous?" Mandy asked.

"Yes, I am, but I'm excited, too. I can't believe it."

The door opened, and Abby was escorted in by Hope. They both looked absolutely stunning. Hope's hair was left down in its long naturally curled locks. Her dress fit her body like it had been painted on.

"Here's your little munchkin. She's ready for her flower girl duties," Hope said with a smile. She really was a beautiful woman.

"Mommy!" Abby ran over to me and wrapped her arms around my neck before kissing my cheek.

"Hi, baby." I picked Abby up and set her on my lap. "Thank you so much, Hope."

"Aw, anytime. You know she's no problem at all." She blew a kiss to Abby. "Skylar, on the other hand, is a handful." We both laughed. "You look so beautiful, Nikki. I'm really happy for you both." My eyes prickled, and my sight was blurred by tears lingering just inside my eyes. She gave a quick wave and ducked back out through the door.

I lifted Abby off my lap. We all gushed over how pretty she was. Her dress fit her perfectly and she looked like a little angel in her white dress with the pink ribbon around her waist. Hope had fixed her hair and left it in large ringlet curls that fell past her shoulders. I hadn't been able to get Bianca, my niece, to walk down with her because my darling brother Gary couldn't guarantee when they'd get in town. My beautiful baby girl was going to be on her own today.

The planner opened the door again. "It's getting close to time, ladies. Nikki, are you ready?"

I took in a deep breath. "Yes, I'm ready." When I stood, I got so dizzy I nearly fell back over. Thanks to my mom grabbing me by the arm, I managed to stay upright.

"Sweetie, are you okay?"

"Yes, I'm fine, Mom. I'm a little tired; I don't think I slept too well last night." I was becoming an expert at lying to cover my dizziness and occasional nausea.

"Maybe you should start taking vitamins or something." Georgia made the suggestion, and I just shrugged my shoulders.

"I think I will, thanks." *I was already taking those horse-pill-sized prenatal vitamins.* "We need to get lined up and ready to go." I wanted to get the attention shifted away from me and back to the wedding.

The planner took them all out into the hall. I peeked out at them through a small space in the doorway made by my foot holding the door open. They all looked so beautiful, so perfect. She paired a bridesmaid with a groomsman as I had instructed for them to be set up. Jackie and Connor would lead off, since she was the Maid of Honor and he was the Best Man. Next would be Sandy and Mandy. I paired them because I thought it was funny their names rhymed. Following them was Hunter and Georgia, and finally, Jorge and Candace.

The music changed once again to the song we knew was the signal to begin the walk down the walkway. This was it, it was show time.

My Dad hadn't made it to the ceremony to walk me down the aisle, but I wasn't surprised. I had planned on my step-dad Jim doing the honor all along. Sine Dad and Mom had divorced, Dad had kept his distance from Gary and me, as well. I had tried to invite him to events in the past, but he'd always decline. I was shocked when he accepted the invitation to come to my wedding. Now, it looked like he was going to be a no-show, again.

Abby protested the walk down the aisle by herself. Let me rephrase that, Abby threw an absolute fit and refused to walk by herself. The planner was at a complete loss. She tried so hard to convince Abby she was a big girl and she could do it, but she was just wasting her breath. Abby refused to walk without holding my hand. It didn't bother me. I wanted her to be part of this day, our day, and she would be. When the wedding march began playing, and it was time for me to walk in with Jim, Abby held my hand on the opposite side from him. Not one flower petal was thrown, but I didn't care. I thought it was even better walking down the aisle holding her little hand. After all, she was a big part of us all, Jeff included now.

Gary sat next to Mom and frowned when our eyes met. I hoped he didn't feel bad because Bianca wasn't able to walk with Abby, or because Abby was walking with me. I loved walking down the aisle holding my little girls hand.

My mom swooped Abby up, causing her to screech, then laugh, when we made it almost all the way to the gazebo.

I had been so distracted by Abby, I hadn't gotten a good look at Jeff until now. When our eyes connected, I knew marrying him was right. After Jim handed me over, Jeff assisted me with getting up the steps onto the platform beside him. He held my hand and my gaze. I mouthed *I love you* to him. He smiled and did the same back. My heart fluttered. He had never mouthed or said those three words to me before. My smile widened across my face as the tears streamed freely.

The great thing about the justice of the peace was the ceremony wasn't dragged out. The longest part was the exchanging of our vows. We both poured our hearts out to each other in front of our family and closest friends. I could have screamed my love for him from the highest mountain to the world. My tears flowed throughout the entire ceremony, and Jeff continued to wipe them away for me with a tissue he drew out of his pocket.

Finally, the words I had been waiting to hear were uttered by the officiant, "I now pronounce you husband and wife. Jeff, you may kiss your bride."

I was pulled gently into his arms, my body fitting perfectly against his chest. He held a finger under my chin as he tipped my head up, our eyes locked on each other. He smiled.

Then he whispered, "I love you, Mrs. Carrington." His warm mouth skimmed mine, before he splayed his hand on my back, pulling me in tighter to him, taking my mouth while not allowing me to even reply. I was lost in him and knew he could feel through my kiss what I hadn't had a chance to say in return, *I love you, too.*

Chapter 8

When we finished taking our photos, we all stood outside the doorway to the grand ballroom. Almost all of our guests had already gone in. The planner doubled as our master of ceremony to introduce the wedding party. We were all talking and laughing. Jackie and Jeff were actually getting along really well. My little Abby was playing with my curls as I held her on my hip.

Jackie and Connor had put together a slide show to display on a huge screen as our guests made their way to the ballroom, got their seating information, and mingled during the cocktail hour. Jackie had used a lot of pictures from my phone and some of Jeff we were able to convince his mom to let us use.

Jackie had also taken a lot of pictures at the rehearsal and during the dinner. I had a chance to see it a few minutes of the slides on my laptop while we were in the hotel, but none of us saw it as it was playing. We could only hear the oohs and ahhs coming from the ballroom as the cocktail hour was coming to an end. Jackie promised we'd each get a copy on DVD, along with the playlist from the reception.

Jeff's mom had a chair to sit on while we waited for the introductions to begin. Her nurse, Karen, was by her side, ready to walk out with her.

"Are you doing okay, Mom?" Jeff asked as he held her hand in his. Watching how affectionate he was with her warmed my heart.

"I'm fine, just a little tired."

"Let me know if you need anything, Mrs. Carrington." I rubbed her back. I had spent time with his mom each week since we first met. I needed her to know me. I wanted her to welcome me to the family and like me.

"I will. I'm very happy to have you as a daughter-in-law, sweetheart." She looked up and smiled at me. *Great, just great. Cue the tears, a-fucking-gain.* Jeff handed me a tissue.

"Our family is growing, Mom," Jeff said. My head snapped toward him, and my mouth fell open. *Jesus fucking Christ.* Everyone seemed to stop their conversations and looked at us. "I meant Nikki has joined the family, and Abby; now there are four of us on my side. What is wrong with you all? What did you think I meant?"

"I knew what you meant, Jeffrey." His mom smiled at us. It amused me that she called him Jeffrey, not Jeff.

Everyone resumed talking, and the planner's assistant came back to let us know we would get started in a few minutes. She was keeping everything on time, just the way I liked it.

Suddenly we heard keys jingling, and we all looked down the hall to see my dad jogging toward us. My mom's smile fell. She looked shocked. Jim put his arm around her shoulder and pulled her into his body. She knew I had invited him, but I'm sure she had thought he'd fail to show, like he had so many times in the past.

"Sorry I'm late, Nikki." He was out of breath. "I wanted to get here for the wedding, but I was held up by work."

"It's okay."

"No, it isn't. I owe you an explanation. I owe you so much more than that. I hope one day you can forgive me."

"I already have forgiven you, Dad." His eyes were wet with tears that wouldn't fall. I didn't want him to be sad or cry. I needed everybody to fucking stay happy so *I* wouldn't cry. Why didn't they understand that? I rubbed his arm, then gave him a one-armed hug.

"We are celebrating today, Dad. No sadness. We will talk and catch up when I get back from the honeymoon. I'm just so glad you made it."

His eyes lit up, and he nodded his head at me.

The assistant adjusted her headset and then let us know it was time for the introductions. I made sure she knew to have my dad introduced after Mom and Jim. We had four specific songs set to play before our first dance. The first two songs were to play at the end of the slideshow. The introductions were to begin on the third song and they should finish just before the fourth song ended. As soon as the fourth song ended, Jeff and I should be introduced, then we would be ready for the first dance. We were using music to cue us.

We wanted Jeff's mom to go first, so she could sit down in a more comfortable seat as everyone else was introduced. Jeff helped her to stand, then hugged her, and gave her a kiss on her forehead. When her name was announced, she began her walk out to the head table, followed closely by Karen.

Mom and Jim were introduced next. They each kissed me, Mom kissed Jeff's cheek, and Jim shook his hand before they walked through the doorway toward their seats. Abby had wanted to go with Mom, but Jeff and I really wanted her to walk in with us, so I held her until they cleared the door before I set her down on the chair.

Next up was my dad. It was awkward as he gave me a kiss and shook Jeff's hand. He didn't even know Jeff. He had never met him before today. I could see his own discomfort flash across his face as he withdrew his hand. I told him he was sitting next to Jeff's mom and Karen, which would put him on the opposite end of the table from Mom and Jim, then he disappeared through the doorway.

Next was the bridal party. They all were in order and paired like they had been when they walked down the aisle earlier. One by one, the couples were introduced, and they walked into the room to loud cheers.

Jeff pulled me into his arms, my back tight against his chest and his arms snaked around my waist. I leaned my head back against him and closed my eyes. This was where I belonged. He lowered his head and inhaled, then blew his warm breath out. I felt the heat on my scalp, and every fiber in my body ignited. This was perfect, he was my heaven.

"Are you happy, baby doll?"

"I've never been happier."

Jeff gently turned me by my shoulders to face him, then lowered his mouth on mine. I could taste his minty breath. With my eyes closed and his mouth consuming mine, I saw stars, the moon, unicorns and all kinds of fantastical things. I was so into him. I grabbed his jacket by the lapels and pulled him closer to me. His kiss was melting me from the inside out. He pressed me back against the wall, with his hands resting on each side of me. I could hear Abby humming in the background and her feet kicking the chair. Our mouths never parted.

The planner announced for us to walk out, but we were lost in each other. The assistant walked back, opening the door. She cleared her throat. *Bitch, please, this is our fucking day*, I thought. Jeff and I smiled as our lips remained touching. I heard the music stop, and I gasped as our mouths parted.

"Mrs. Carrington, it's time for us to get this party started." He wiped around my lips. "Lipstick is smudged a bit." He smiled and held his hand out for me. Our fingers intertwined, and Jeff nodded at the assistant, indicating we were ready. I signaled for Abby to join us and held her hand in mine.

I squeezed his hand, and he looked down at me. "I love you, babe." My heart felt like it had swollen three sizes larger, like the Grinch's on Christmas.

"I love you, too."

We heard the planner announce us: "Ladies and gentlemen, I now present to you, Mr. and Mrs. Jeffrey Carrington, and Abby."

We walked out to a standing ovation and loud cheers. As expected, my waterworks were flowing once again. Abby pulled free of me and took off in the direction of Gary and his family. We walked right out onto the dance floor, and our first song, *Here and Now*, began to play. I knew that song; I had heard Jackie playing it several times. Jackie knew what the first dance song was going to be, but she had refused to tell me. Jeff had picked it. I smiled as I thought what lengths he had to go to for her to stay silent. He must have threatened her. "*Here in my heart, I believe your love is all I'll ever need.*" Let the tears begin. I looked up toward Jeff and was surprised to see he had a lone tear rolling down his cheek. My fingers wiped it away, then slowly trailed down his face. He was mine. We were one. He was everything I ever needed.

Jeff sang the entire song to me. I cried more tears than I had thought humanly possible. Every time he uttered the words, *your love is all I need*, he gave me a little squeeze. He lifted my face so our eyes met when the song was close to ending. "God, I love you, Nikki." Another tear eased down his face as he lowered his mouth onto mine. Our mouths, our hearts, our lives were fused together.

When the song ended, our kiss didn't. We stood on the floor, bound together by our love, as everyone clapped. We struggled to break away from each other as the planner announced that we would have a few words from Jim and my dad, then dinner would be served. We walked around and took our places at the head table. I couldn't keep my hands off him. I let my hand caress his arm from shoulder to wrist, then stroked his muscular thigh under the table.

Jeff leaned in and whispered to me, "Baby doll, there is nothing I'd love more than to bury my cock in you right now and feel your heat wrapped around me. I'm doing everything in my power to keep from clearing this fucking table and taking you right here. You aren't helping me any when you touch me like that." He placed his hand on mine and stilled it.

Jim made his speech, and after everyone applauded him, the microphone was handed to my dad. "This ought to be interesting," I mumbled under my breath. I looked out, and my eyes met with Gary's. I watched him as he stood from his table and walked over near the door to leave the ballroom. I knew he despised our dad and that would never change.

Dad did himself and all of us a favor; he kept it very short and to the point. I was concerned he would embarrass himself, then embarrass me. Instead, he wished Jeff and me well, said he was looking forward to getting to know Jeff, and said he was proud of me. I think he was reaching for anything to say at that point. He didn't know exactly what he was proud of, but he was proud. *If he can't name at least one thing, then who gives many fucks? Not me, not today.*

I was so hungry by the time my plate was set in front of me, I ate everything, I didn't care. I was still hungry. I caught myself looking at the food that had been left on everyone else's plate and wondered how greedy I would look if I ate what they weren't going to. I couldn't do it, but I sure wanted to.

As the plates were being cleared, it was time to begin the toasts. First up was Connor. As he stood, I saw a slight problem. He swayed back and forth a little as he raised his glass and took the microphone. As he started talking, his voice was strong and he was able to talk over the clanking of plates and silverware being collected. A couple minutes in, his volume faded and he was barely audible, then, out of nowhere, his voice boomed loud again. He did this several times, where he drifted off, then his inflection was loud again. Jeff and I were annoyed, but chuckled at him.

Hunter had had enough. He told Connor to wrap that shit up, causing the entire room to roar with laughter. Finally, Connor raised his glass and concluded, "I love you guys. May you have many happy years together." We all clapped, mostly because he was done, and he handed the microphone to Jackie. Jeff slid his arm behind me along the chair back, then rubbed his fingertips lightly across my shoulder. Goosebumps raised all over my skin.

"I'll keep my toast short and sweet, unlike Connor." Everyone laughed again. "Nikki is like a sister to me; we've known each other for years. I love you, girl. And Jeff, welcome to the family." She winked and her voice cracked. She took a deep breath and exhaled slowly. "Jeff and Nikki, here's to you. I love you both." I knew the tears were the reason she stopped. Jackie didn't cry, and to see her so emotional was unraveling me. Jeff handed me another napkin.

She walked down to us, instead of sitting, and gave us both a hug. I loved her so much. She whispered, "You guys are going to love this next song." She patted Jeff's shoulder, then went back to her seat.

Our planner came and retrieved the microphone, which was probably a good idea since it had been laid on the table next to Connor. She was really keeping things humming along at a good pace. "Next up, we have another dance for our newlyweds. This is a special request from the maid of honor, Jackie, to the happy couple, Jeff and Nikki."

We both rose from our seats. Jeff laced his fingers through mine, and we made our way to the dance floor. The music began, and my body swayed with the beat as I listened hard to the words. Jackie was a musical genius. This song was so perfect. It was another song I had heard her play several times recently but never thought anything about it. She had been giving away our songs in the last few weeks without telling me. I had memorized parts of the song after hearing it so many times. Jeff held me tight as I began singing aloud. He looked at me with one of his eyebrows raised.

"*I need your love, I need it now, baby,*" I sang. *"The way you love me, the way you love me."* My gaze met his. "*You make me feel like I'm alive, baby. You make my temperature rise high, sugar."* My body broke out in goose bumps. Oh my god, this song was made for us. "*I need your love, I need it now, baby."* The goose flesh wouldn't go away. Jeff asked if I was cold, but I wasn't. I was just so in love, and this song was love personified. It said everything I felt. Our bodies were in sync, we were locked together, moving back and forth to the incredible beat. *The way you love me makes me feel that something that I never felt before, and I can't imagine life without you anymore.* His hands held my face, and there was no space between us; each movement Jeff made, my body instinctively followed him. His mouth lowered onto mine, his tongue glided between my lips to meet mine. *And sugar, furthermore, I'm going to love you till forever.* Pure genius.

As we walked off the floor, Jackie was waiting for us. "I have all of these songs on a CD for you guys. What'd you think?"

"I loved it; you are amazing." I gave her a hug around her neck and kissed her cheek. "She has an amazing voice, and the words of that song were perfect."

"You can't go wrong with Teena Marie," Jeff said with a huge smile and gave her a hug. She had a shocked look on her face when he released her.

We were interrupted when the planner began her next announcement. "Time for the next dance; this one is Jim and Nikki, and Jeff and Rebekka." The planner was really cracking the whip to stay on schedule. We really did want to hurry up and open the dance floor to everyone, though.

"Have fun, kids." Jackie laughed and went back to her seat.

Jeff and I walked back out to the dance floor, where we were joined by Mom and Jim. The plan for the dances with parents was that we would dance for a little while, then switch partners so Jeff and I ended up finishing the dance together.

I knew once the song began, that Connor hadn't had a lot of input into these first few songs. Jeff and I held each other's gaze for the first few stanzas of the song. He winked at me, right as the words *you made my heart your home* followed shortly by *there's no one else for me* were crooned. He picked this. I didn't know how he had come to like such provocative music, but I loved it. The words, the melody, everything about this day. I felt like I had won at life. He mouthed at me 'I love you' right as the words *I know where my happiness is, now that I have you ... And you have me, forever* were sang out.

Yep, you guessed it, more fucking tears.

As Jim and I danced, he told me how happy he was for me. He knew I'd find the right man and, when everyone else didn't think so, he had believed Jeff was the one. He really liked Jeff. I gave him a hug, he was on my side all along. I knew it.

We switched partners and finished dancing the rest of the song with our soul mates. Everyone clapped and cheered when the song ended. Jeff and I were wrapped in each other's arms once again.

The planner tapped the microphone, and we put a little space between us. There would be plenty of time for that later. "I hear you guys are heading to Hawaii for ten days. Have a safe and happy trip. We have one more dance before we open the floor. This one is for Jeff and his mother, Lisa, and Nikki and her dad."

We hadn't walked too far off the floor this time, and my dad, surprisingly, helped Lisa walk out to Jeff. He won a few points with me for that. The song began, and I could tell from the music intro, it was the same singer that Jackie had picked for the other song.

Dad had approached me timidly; he was nervous and felt uneasy. It had been so many years. We didn't talk at first, we just danced, and I listened to the words of the song. Jackie knew good and damn well who I'd be dancing with when she picked this song. The words were so telling of my feelings, but I just smiled at Dad. My heart began to beat faster than the normal pace. He had me spinning around, just like the words said. I'm out on a limb. I glanced over at Jeff. He and his mom were smiling at each other, enjoying the dance. *Yep, I'm out on a limb for sure.* There was no way I was going to switch and interrupt Jeff dancing with his mom.

I had to break this uncomfortable silence. "Thanks for coming, Dad. It means a lot to me."

When my dad looked at me, his eyes were wet. He managed to choke out, "I love you, Nikki. I'm so sorry I hurt you."

Yep, I'm a sucker for my dad. I'm giving in to him and am definitely out on a limb. I rested my head on his shoulder, and we danced in silence until the song ended. I had tears slide down my face, following the crease of my nose. Before we left the floor, I kissed his cheek and told him I loved him.

The next song began and Jeff held my hand to lead me onto the dance floor. We stood on the floor, his arms held me tight to him. It was a faster song, intended for everyone to join in with us. I peeked around Jeff's arm at the planner to see what she was doing. Just as our eyes met, she made the announcement. "Everyone, please, join Jeff and Nikki for this dance." Within a matter of seconds the floor was packed. Everyone danced, and those closest to us came over to congratulate us, again.

We walked off the floor, when that song ended. The planner seemed almost giddy as she announced for everyone to stay on the dance floor. Immediately, they went to line dancing with The Electric Slide.

I sat next to Jeff as we watched everyone go through their own version of the dance steps. Mom and Jim were out there dancing. Mom had taken Abby out on the dance floor, too. Karen had gone out on the dance floor. Jackie, Hunter, Georgia, and Connor were having the best time of everyone, it seemed. The only four from the head table not dancing were me and Jeff, his mom, and my dad. The two of them sat and chatted on the far end of the table, occasionally smiling up our direction.

"My feet are starting to hurt."

"Kick your shoes off and leave them under the table so you can find them later."

"If I take them off, they won't go back on. I think my feet are swelling. The shoes are new, and I didn't break them in."

"That sucks." Jeff leaned down and lifted my feet into his lap. Behind the table, he massaged my calves and ankles. *Yes, he was my slice of heaven.* We talked, kissed, and talked some more.

After about an hour of dancing, the planner announced it was time for the cake cutting. That was pretty uneventful, in the grand scheme of everything else today. I had no intention of smashing a piece of cake into Jeff's face, and I knew he wouldn't do that to me. We took our pictures, and the cake was served to everyone. We had the embossed bags for those who wanted to take their piece home. Instead of the dancing resuming right away, we tossed the garter and bouquet. I kept an eye on Abby, who was having a great time running around with Bianca.

Instead of sitting down, I decided I had to get out of those shoes. My feet were killing me. I stood to walk to the dressing area, and Jeff followed me. We both were ready to get changed. We made our way back to the dressing rooms when Jeff pulled me by my arm, nearly toppling me over, into the room with him.

"Damn, baby, I've been waiting to get a few minutes alone with you."

I was pulled in close to him. His faint smell of cologne mingled with his own unique scent was intoxicating. "This feels so good, being in your arms. Being your wife."

Jeff reached over and locked the door.

"What are you doing?"

"I just need a few minutes with you, that's all."

I could feel his need pressing into my stomach. I wanted to feel him in me so bad, but I knew that couldn't happen, not here. That's all that had consumed my mind from the time we walked down the aisle to the gazebo.

"What if we get caught?"

"We're on the guys' side; trust me, they'll understand. And we're married, what is anyone going to say?" His hands touched my hair, while his eyes looked wildly at the ponytail holder and comb. I could sense his desire to rip my hair down so he could run his fingers through it, grab a handful, and then pull me into him. "Just be quiet. I need to taste you, baby."

"It's got to be quick, and I'll be quiet." I hiked my dress up around my waist revealing my soaked panties. I had wanted to wear a thong, but the thought of changing in front of my mother in it didn't seem appropriate.

"I can smell your beautiful pussy begging for my cock." Jeff ran his hand between my legs across the wet material, then held his fingers up under his nose, inhaling my scent. "Damn, baby, this is the fuck-me scent I love so much." He reached under the waistband of my panties, wrapped it around his fingers, and yanked hard, stripping me of it with one tug.

There was a ledge in the room that he lifted me onto, then pressed my legs apart. My body lurched to catch myself from falling off. His tongue lapped at my core.

I moaned out. "Jesus, Jeff."

He raised his eyes to meet mine. How fucking hot was this? Looking down at his gorgeous face, my husband, peering at me over my mound while feasting on my clit. He licked down between my folds, then back up and sucked on my nub, sending desire through my body. I wanted to feel him in me. I needed to feel him in me.

He slid two fingers in my pussy and fingered me as he sucked and nipped at my clit. My hips moved slightly to meet his strokes. The beard hairs made me crazy. I loved the roughness pressing into my flesh. "Damn," I panted out. My fingers dug into his hair, running my nails across his scalp. He dragged his digits in and out of my core, sending me over the edge. I gasped then squealed out. I wasn't quiet. He stood and clasped his hand over my mouth. "Baby, I told you, you have to be quiet."

"You do this to me. I wanted to be quiet, but what the hell." I knew we couldn't be back there too much longer before someone came looking for us. He pulled me into him. I could taste me on his lips. When he released me, I held onto his shoulders and hopped off the ledge.

"You could have asked for help to get down. I don't want you to get hurt." His glare was firm, holding me in place as his eyes scolded me.

I reached to unfasten his belt. "I knew I could get down." I unzipped his pants and slid them down, releasing him to me. His cock bounced and jutted out, waiting for my mouth to provide the release he wanted.

The floor was hard, but I didn't care. I planned to to suck his cock so fucking good; I wasn't going to have to be down on my knees for long. I lashed out my tongue to lick the drops from his exposed, swollen crown, then jetted my tongue along the underside before I took him in my mouth. I moaned out, followed by his moan.

I tugged to make sure my dress wasn't under my knees and continued my attack of him. I was hungry for him. I massaged him at the base as my mouth worked his length. "God damn, Nikki." He pushed my head to take him deeper. I did my best but had to pull back when I felt myself begin to gag. I held his sack with my hand when he took control and began massaging himself, thrusting in and out of my mouth. I could tell it wouldn't be long, and I was ready. I knew there was no way he could come on me right now. I was going to have to swallow every single drop, and I wanted to swallow his nectar. I loved drinking him down, feeling his hot seed spurt into my mouth, and be gulped down my throat. He tasted so good.

It only took him a few more thrusts before he grabbed my head and held me in place to take all of him. I wrapped my mouth around and sucked him until the last drop was drained. I licked his shaft and base to make sure there was no remaining trace of his sweet juice. I wanted it all. I loved him so much. I couldn't get enough of him.

He placed his hand on my head, tipping it back so I was looking up into his heated dark eyes. "I love you, baby doll." He pulled me up into his embrace.

"I love you, too." He held me for a few minutes as I licked my tongue across my lips, still savoring the taste of him mixed with the faint taste of myself.

He released me from his grip, then helped me pull my dress down to cover me. I ducked into my dressing room and changed, while he did the same. I had one small problem now: no underwear.

Chapter 9

My mind flashed back to the day before, our wedding day. I was still floating. Remembering Jeff singing to me, feeling him hold me close, and hearing him tell me he loved me -- those three words had been stated several times, clearly, as he looked into my eyes -- my dreams had come true. I melted into him on the dance floor. We were married, and I loved him more than I ever thought was possible.

We were about to embark on our ten-day adventure. For the past month, I had been online almost daily to learn as much as possible about the Hawaiian Islands we were going to visit. I knew before we left that a return trip would be required. There was so much to see and do, but our honeymoon wasn't planned to be a complete tourist trip. We had a couple things planned that we absolutely wanted to on this trip, but most of our time was going to be spent wrapped in each other's arms. I couldn't think of anywhere else in the universe I wanted to be.

"Baby, are you ready? We have to get moving." I could hear Jeff's footsteps getting louder as he approached the bedroom doorway.

I took one more glance at myself in the mirror. I had on a white tank top and a pair of navy blue linen shorts that reached mid-thigh. Knowing I was going through security, I wore my white platform flip-flops. I stuffed an oversized navy and white striped button down sweater in my carry-on.

"Almost; let me grab the last few things from the bathroom and I'll be done." I pointed at the larger suitcase sitting near the door. "You can take that bag." I took in his stunning form near leaning against the molding of the doorway. He was beyond gorgeous in his Affliction jeans that fit him perfectly. The Affliction T-shirt clung to his biceps and powerful torso like a second skin. If it was even possible to be jealous of that shirt, I was.

He bent to pick up the suitcase, then set it back down. "You know there's a weight limit, right? Because I think you've exceeded it." He laughed, then picked the suitcase back up and headed downstairs.

I didn't care about the weight limit. I had things I had to have and things I wanted just in case. I thought I had done a pretty good job packing, considering the length of time we would be away. Jeff got all of our luggage loaded up in the car, and then we were ready to get underway. Jeff locked up the house, we got situated in the car, and we were on our way to Tampa International.

I had three things I was looking forward to more than anything. First, was to finally be able to eat without the concern that my gown wouldn't fit. Second, was having ten days away from everyone to relax, clear my head and unwind. I'd miss Abby like crazy, but I knew, between my mom and Sky, she was in very loving and capable hands. And lastly, I was looking forward to every precious moment alone with Jeff.

"I am so happy, baby doll."

"Me too. I love you so much."

"I love you more. I can't wait to get you in that hotel room."

"I would have thought you got enough of me last night."

"Never that." His devilish smirk flashed on his face.

A smile crept up on my face. "Which island are we going to first?"

"The big island first."

"I'm so excited. But this long flight is going to suck."

"Hopefully you remembered your Kindle. I have my trusty iPod right here." He tapped his jeans pocket.

We pulled into long-term parking. A shuttle drove around and met us right beside our car. The driver helped Jeff get our luggage on board. He handed Jeff a ticket before climbing back in his seat and driving to pick up another couple. My eyes were fixed on Jeff as he looked out the window. *How did I get so lucky?* I loved him so much. He turned and looked at me with a smirk on his face. He leaned in to me, his arm brushing against my breast, and my nipple responded and hardened. His warm breath kissed my face as he told me how badly he wanted me and what he was planning to do to me later, before slanting his lips on mine. The kiss was soft and sensual.

We arrived at the terminal. He and the driver got all of our luggage off the shuttle, we checked our bags at the curbside counter, then grabbed our carry-ons before heading to security. I breezed through without any hassle. Jeff was not so lucky. He was scanned, rescanned, and eventually patted down. I stood watching and chuckling at him; his lips were pinched together, and he shook his head in disgust.

"That was so not funny, Mrs. Carrington." I still wasn't used to being called Mrs. Carrington, but I loved the way it sounded. It was music to my ears.

"I think she just wanted to cop a feel. She lingered a little too long on your hips and ass."

"Fucking TSA." He smiled at me as he motioned with his head toward the gift shop. "Do you want anything? A water or soda?"

"A water and a Snickers, please." I was craving chocolate.

"Sure thing, doll. I'll be right back." He ducked inside the gift shop and emerged a few minutes later with a bag. He reached in the bag and pulled out what he'd bought. "I got us each one."

"Thanks, but I was planning to use you."

"Beautiful, you can use me however you see fit. But you'll appreciate this soft neck pillow a lot more than my not-so-soft shoulder before we land." He stood before me, squeezing it.

Our time away was going to be awesome. Or scheduled wasn't going to be crammed with things to do, like I had originally intended. Instead, I took Jeff's advice and found one thing I absolutely wanted to do on each island and wrote that down. If we did more, that was great, but there was no pressure to run around like we had to do everything in one trip. He assured me we would come back every year if I wanted.

We got lucky on the flight, too. There were a lot of connecting flights, but we managed to get a non-stop trip. It sucked that it was ten hours, but at least we were in first class.

Once we got boarded on the plane, I had a hard time getting comfortable. I fidgeted and wiggled around so much, I drew the attention of the flight attendants.

"Ma'am, is everything okay? Can I get you anything?"

"She's pregnant; she's okay," Jeff said with a huge smile on his face. I slapped his arm.

"What the hell? Why would you tell her that?"

"Did I lie?"

"No, but still."

"Baby, you're probably going to be way more uncomfortable before we land. It was better they know the truth than try to bullshit them."

"I'm just …"

"You're just what? Pregnant? Irritated? Hormonal? Yeah, guess what -- I know."

I sat back and just shook my head. "Will you get me my Kindle, please?"

He stood, and his junk was at eye level. I felt the dampness down there. *Jeez, I'm a fucking sex fiend*, I thought. I immediately thought how random and erotic it would be to rip his pants off and slam his cock down my throat in front of the over two hundred forty passengers on the plane. I could imagine the gray-haired women gasping for oxygen, just mortified, while the young folks would be all kinds of turned on. *What the hell? Why am I having thoughts like this?*

When Jeff sat in his seat, that thought evaporated, but the uncomfortable wetness was still lingering. I drank the last of my water and stuck the bottle in the seat pocket in front of me as we got ready for take-off.

After sitting in my seat reading for nearly half an hour, I could barely keep my eyes open. I closed my Kindle and leaned against Jeff's arm with my eyes closed. The heat felt so good coming from him. My thoughts were instantly drawn back to our reception.

We'd had an unbelievable time. Jackie and Connor, well, technically Jeff and not so much Connor, had done great with the music selections. It was so nice watching everyone dancing and laughing, having a good time. And then the dressing room, *damn*!

Jeff shook me.

"What?" I opened my eyes and glared at him.

He leaned into me and whispered into my ear. "You're moaning."

"No way." I clasped my hand over my mouth. I hadn't meant to do it, it just happened. The thought of the day before was so hat and fresh in my mind, I couldn't help myself.

"I shit you not. The same moaning as when I'm fucking you."

I could feel the heat rise into my cheeks. They had to be beet red. "I was thinking about yesterday, in the dressing room."

I heard the growl rumble in his throat. I noticed my panties were damp, again, when I shifted in my seat.

I felt like I was turning into a nymphomaniac. I couldn't get enough of him. I flipped up the divider between us and snuggled closer to him, pulling his arm around me. I closed my eyes again.

I heard a flight attendant ask if we wanted anything to drink. My throat was parched. I used Jeff's arm to help sit up, but accidentally dug my nails in his flesh.

"Hey, be careful." He grabbed my fingers.

"I'm sorry, I was trying to pull myself up."

"What's wrong?"

"I just need some ginger ale."

"Do you feel all right?"

"Yeah, just thirsty."

I got my drink, then opened my Kindle to resume reading my book. It didn't take long before I found myself fighting to keep my eyes open again.

I was freezing and asked Jeff to get my sweater for me. Instead of putting it on, I draped it over my body. I laid against him again, his arm wrapped around me, and his hand found its resting place on my breast, his fingers strumming across my hardened nipple. I wrapped my arms around his waist on top of the seat belt. His caressing made my desire rise. *Fuck, what about him **didn't** make my desire rise?* I kissed his chest over the T-shirt, and I heard him hiss through his teeth as he exhaled. I pulled my sweater down to cover his crotch and ran my hands gently over him. I wanted him but I couldn't have him. My body was craving him. My wanton strokes were halted when he grabbed my wrist. "You need to stop, now."

I peered up into his beautiful lust-filled eyes. He wanted me, too. "Okay, for now." I shifted myself and sat up. He pulled me up onto his lap, swallowing my frame in his muscular arms. I could feel his semi-hard bulge beneath me. He pulled the sweater over my shoulder and rested his hand on my swollen, hard nipple again, thumbing, caressing, and pinching it. He wasn't playing fair. He could tease me, but I couldn't touch him. I felt like a flood was taking place in my panties, I was so wet with need. *More like wet with greed.*

He held me for a few minutes with my head resting on his shoulder. I could hear the music through his iPod. My breathing had changed to panting under his fondling. He was torturing me. He slid his finger up to my mouth, and I pulled them in, silently sucking, like I was sucking his cock. I felt the rumble of his moan that he had strained to not let anyone hear. I pulled the entire length of his digit into my mouth, then sucked against his attempt to drag it slowly back out. He ran his hand down my hair, giving me a slight tug. I lifted my head, and our eyes met. The heat that was coming off both of us could have set a fire. He pulled me into him and took ownership of my mouth.

His hand slid down my chest again, skimming over my stomach, then resting on my bare thigh; *not a good idea Mr. Carrington. Touch me there and I'm going to come undone in your arms, right here, right now, on this plane.* He gently slid his hand up and down my thigh, then stopped. He whispered to me, "Your little moans and whimpers are driving me insane. We have to stop. I can't take much more of this."

"Probably a good idea. I want you so bad right now, it hurts," I whispered in his ear.

"You're going to get every bit of me buried in your hot pussy when we get to our room." He grabbed a handful of my hair and pulled me into him, his tongue reaching deeper into my mouth than ever before. He broke the kiss. "God damn, Nikki, what you do to me." He pushed me off him onto my own seat. "Stay in your seat, beautiful. You're way too dangerous to be on my lap."

I looked down and saw the wet spot on his jeans. I desperately wanted to lick it.

Jeff helped me get the neck pillow situated so I could try to get some rest. I feared we'd land and I'd be too tired to do anything.

After about an hour of sleep, I woke and noticed Jeff staring at me. I rubbed my hand across his bearded chin. "What's wrong?"

"Nothing, baby, just admiring you."

I could feel the heat flush to my cheeks. We had a quick discussion about how to handle things when we returned. We expected to get bombarded with questions from everyone about the trip, pictures, what we did and didn't do. Plus, we had a big announcement to make. We decided the best way to thank everyone for making our wedding day so special was to have a party at the house the Saturday after we returned home. We could also share pictures and stories. But most importantly, we would make the announcement that we were expecting a baby to everyone at the same time.

I was so happy when we touched down on the island and got off that plane. After we landed, we sent a text to everyone, including Jim and Mom, so they all knew we made it safely, and so they would have plenty of notice for our return party. Our honeymoon was finally ready to begin.

Chapter 10

My mouth hung open as Jeff drove the rental car out into the Hawaiian beauty. I had never seen such fantastic scenery. Hawaii was amazing, or what I had seen so far was. We didn't drive very long before he turned into the four-star resort driveway and followed the signs up to the front desk for check-in. We were three hours earlier than the normal check-in time.

We were met by the friendliest staff I had ever seen. The gentleman helped Jeff unload our luggage onto the cart, walked us in to the front desk, where we were checked-in without any delay, then he assisted us with getting everything up into our room. Okay, I know they are supposed to do all of that because they want a tip, but this young man's demeanor was very gracious.

It hadn't been a full day, and already, I missed my little munchkin. I felt more at ease being away from Abby for so long after Hope agreed to stay with Sky and help him. He was a wonderful father, and I knew he was more than capable of taking care of her, but his job had him working weird hours. Mom also offered to help as much as her schedule allowed. She was a lucky little girl; she had so many people who loved her. As Jeff and the bellman took care of the luggage, I made a quick phone call to Sky and talked to Abby briefly while I walked through the room.

Our room was fantastic and super spacious. It was like being in an apartment. A large apartment. We were in the presidential suite. There were two super large bedrooms, each with a four post canopied king-sized bed; and two full spa-like bathrooms and a half bath. The living room and dining room exterior walls were made of glass, providing a wonderful view of the water and beaches, even if you stood in the kitchen. There was a separate room that had a grand piano. The decorations were exquisite. We had private balconies, with outdoor seating accessible from nearly every room.

I couldn't wait to explore the rest of the hotel. When the front desk told us there were twelve restaurants, twelve bars, three pools, and a waterslide, and that the resort sat on sixty-two acres of oceanfront property, I was stunned. We really, technically, didn't need to leave here to find something to do.

Jeff closed the door behind the bellman after handing him a tip. I was so excited to be there, I ran to him and wrapped my arms around his neck. He lifted me, and my legs instinctively wrapped around his waist. Our lips crashed together. He held me to him tight, with his arms low across my hips and ass. I could feel the wetness as our kiss deepened.

I dropped my legs from around his waist and loosened my hands from his neck. I grabbed his hands and pulled him over to the window in the living room.

"Look at this view, baby! This is so beautiful. It's like we're in heaven."

"Being anywhere with you is heaven, baby doll."

His hand grasped me by the hair at my nape and pulled me toward him. His tongue sank between my lips as I eagerly opened for him. Jeff leaned down, not removing his mouth from mine, swooped me up into his arms, and carried me into one of the bedrooms. He walked to the bed and laid me down on it, then he laid beside me, pulling me into him. His lips grazed across mine, his tongue slid across mine, and his eyes bored into mine.

With a sigh, he rolled onto his back, pulling me on top of him. Each of his hands grabbed a handful of my hair and held my mouth on his. I loved it. I loved anything he did with or to me. I just didn't wanted him to rip it out, because that would have meant he'd let me go.

He released his grip on my hair, then slid his hands down my shoulders, down my sides, and gripped my hips. My eyes closed as I lost myself to him. His demanding hands wiggled me, and I followed his lead. I gyrated on his hardened length that was straining beneath his jeans. A moan escaped my lips as I tossed my head back, throwing my hair off of my face.

"Jesus fucking Christ, Nikki."

I opened my eyes and our gaze met. His eyes were hooded, and mine had to be screaming and pleading for him to take me. I pushed my knees in tight, pressing into his sides as I slid gently against him, rubbing my clit across the fly of his pants. I needed to be fucked. My hips lifted slightly and moved up so I could feel his swollen head press across my clothed, wet entrance.

I lifted the tank top up and over my head, then struggled a little as it tangled in my hair, but pulled it loose before tossing it onto the floor. Jeff's hips were slowly rising and staying tight against me. He groaned as each of his hands surrounded my covered breasts, kneading, and grazing across my pebbled nipples hidden beneath my bra.

"Stand up," he commanded me. I did as requested. He stood alongside of me, then reached behind me to unhook my bra and removed it, exposing me to him. I reached for his jeans, but he held my wrists. "Not yet, baby." His voice was deep and sultry.

He unbuttoned and unzipped my shorts, then slowly pressed them and my panties down to my ankles. I kicked off my flip-flops and stepped out of my garments, leaving me completely naked in front of him.

"You are so fucking beautiful." He lowered his head to my hardened peak and took it in his mouth. One hand was wrapped around the back of me at my waist, the other was nudging my legs to part, exploring my folds. As a finger dipped into my wetness, I let out a soft mewl and sigh. I was going to fucking come undone just from his touch. A shiver ran through me causing my body to quake.

"Do you need me to adjust the temperature in here?"

"I'm fine. I'm not cold." He should have known his touch drove me insane.

He kissed me gently before resuming his attention to my needy nipple. His fingers continued their exploration of my slick heat. His digits pressed and massaged against my swollen clit as I lifted my foot and placed it on the side rail of the bed. Then, without warning, he stopped.

"You're so ready for me, baby. Stay just like that."

I stood and watched him remove his shirt to reveal his beautiful sculpted abs and chest. He took a step back toward me and kissed my mouth quickly before stepping away from me again. I'm pretty sure I began to drool as he unbuckled his belt, unbuttoned and unzipped his jeans, then stood there, staring at me. I could see his bulge begging for release from the restrictive denim fabric.

"Come here." He summoned me over with his arms outstretched to me.

I yanked my foot down off the rail and practically ran to him like a starving, greedy, wild animal. I thought I was going to fall. He held me in his arms for what seemed like an eternity before giving me the go ahead to help him take his jeans off.

As I slid them down over his hips, his erection sprang free and popped out toward me, teasing me, begging me for a kiss. It took every bit of restraint not to touch him yet. I let out a sigh as I continued to press his jeans down his muscular thighs. I instructed him to have a seat on the edge of the bed, then, one leg at a time, removed his shoes, then I pulled the jeans off over his feet. He tried to stand, but I pressed him back down. It was time I took charge. I'd had enough of his teasing me. I knew what I wanted, and I wanted it right then.

My tongue caressed up his inner thigh. When I reached his testicles, I kissed them gently, before my tongue continued its pursuit of his length, up the underside of his shaft, stroking the thick, inviting vein, then up to the ridge, circling around its thickness, then out to the tip, teasing his slit before engulfing his crown. He hissed his pleasure and growled deep in the back of his throat. My eyes roamed up his beautiful body to see his eyes closed. He was mine.

I worked my mouth up and down his shaft, making sure to tease across the bulbous top before taking him back into my throat. I could feel him harden even more as he began to raise his hips to my mouth. He thrust gently in and out of my mouth. I reached down between my legs and felt the hungry wetness as I rubbed my clit. I cried out and moaned. It took no time for me to find my orgasm before Jeff removed his cock from my mouth.

"Damn, baby," He said as he pulled me up on the bed. "Are you ready for me?"

"Fuck yeah, I'm ready. I've been ready." I scooted my ass back up toward the middle of the bed, but Jeff grabbed my legs and pulled me back across the sheets toward him.

"Not so fast, sweetness." He placed my feet on his shoulders, parted my folds, and inhaled deep. "Damn, I love your smell. I wish there was a way to bottle that scent so I could carry it with me." He took in another deep breath, before his tongue licked down my slickness. He slid one finger in me as his tongue lapped in circles on my clit.

"Damn, baby," I whimpered. My eyes were closed, and I was being pushed near the edge, again.

He growled again, then slid a second finger inside me, massaging deep in my core. I was so close to unraveling. His fingers kept stroking in and out while his tongue was working magic on my button. He picked up speed with his fingers, and I could feel his knuckles slam into my tender flesh.

"God. Damn. It!" I screamed out as I gripped the sheets. "Fuck!" I was squirming and pressing myself into his hand and mouth, writhing as if I were possessed.

"Oh yeah, baby. Come all over me." He was licking and lapping as his fingers continued to slay me. "You taste so fucking sweet."

As I came down from my high, *yeah, I was high, I was fucked up out of my mind with that orgasm,* I felt a cool spot on the bed. *What the hell?*

I raised myself up onto my elbows and noticed a huge wet spot, and Jeff was wiping his mouth off. *Holy shit, please tell me I didn't pee when I came?*

"That was awesome; you squirted again, baby."

"Um ..." I was dumbfounded and embarrassed. I guess if I had known, I could have warned him or something. "I'm sorry."

"Don't ever apologize. I loved it. It's so sweet, tastes heavenly." He stood and climbed up on the bed, kneeling beside me. "Turn and put your head up on the pillows."

I eagerly scrambled to get into position, then spread my legs, inviting him to me. "Don't tease me, please," I pleaded as I massaged him lightly along his outer thighs.

He pushed my ankles back over my head slightly, raising my ass off the bed and exposing my tight knot to him as he rubbed his tip across my inviting, eager hole and ass. *So much for my request.* My slickness was incredible and seemed to make him even harder. He had distributed our comingled lubrication to cover me entirely. He pressed slowly against the tightness of my ass. Holding his length firmly in one hand, he flicked the head back and forth to stimulate me, hoping I wouldn't object. As he continued to rub and poke at me, he again pressed to try to slip into my tight opening.

"Not there." I stopped him and pressed my hand against his thigh to push him back.

"I was just messing around," Jeff said. "Your ass looks so good, so inviting."

"Maybe one day." *One day, like when hell freezes over.*

He stole one final feel with his swollen crest before moving back up to my slit. He let my legs drop back down and placed my feet on his chest before he parted my lips, sinking slowly into me. I arched my back as he sank deeper into me, then I lifted my hips up to meet his, taking him completely. The feeling of him grinding deeper into me, touching against the deepest tissues while rubbing his pubis craftily against my aching clit forced another orgasm from me. My moans became deep sighs.

"Fuck me hard, baby." I just wanted to feel him feverishly pound into me.

He was more than willing to oblige before he gasped out, "I don't know how long I'll last like this." He changed speeds, thrusting hard and furiously, then slowing down to long, deep, sensual plunges before picking up the pace again. "Tell me when you are there again," he uttered to me as he pressed my thighs far apart, widening the gap. His sweat was dripping down onto my stomach and mound. My hands searched his body. They felt around his muscular arms, around his waist, and down his butt, pulling him into me as if I were trying to swallow him up.

"Shit, now," I cried out as my body quaked. Jeff intensified his movements repeatedly until I felt my orgasm rip through me, and simultaneously, he found his release. He collapsed on the bed next to me, wrapping me tightly into his arms. We laid there like that for many minutes. He showered my face with kisses.

We eventually retreated to the shower, then, after brushing our teeth, decided it was time to get something to eat, then find the tram and take a tour of the resort.

Chapter 11

The time in Hawaii flew by. Before I knew it, we were on the return flight, downhearted at the thought of returning to our normal lives. Of course, I was eager to see Abby, our family, and friends, but the time we had spent together had been so blissful.

Our flight landed late Wednesday night. I knew it was too late to get Abby; she had to have been fast asleep. Sky would drop her at day care, then I'd make sure he knew I would pick her up and that I would have her the entire weekend.

After a restful night's sleep in our own familiar bed, we rose and busied ourselves with planning the menu for Saturday's party. We checked with everyone to make sure they were able to make it. I scrambled to compile our pictures that we planned to show everyone into a PowerPoint presentation. We were going to take the laptop down to the movie theater and have the pictures set up to display on the large screen. I inhaled, deep in thought, and exhaled loudly.

"What's bugging you, baby?" Jeff asked. He stood behind me and rubbed my shoulder.

"I was thinking about when we tell them all the baby news. I can just see Mom, Jackie, and probably Georgia's mouths drop to the floor. How are we going to tell them?"

"I hadn't really given it a whole lot of thought. I guess we can just say it."

"I don't know. Well, maybe. Maybe we can find some way to say it really fast."

"That's fine, if that's what you want."

I rubbed my hands across my face. "I don't know what I want."

Jeff stepped closer behind me, his jeans grazing across my upper back. *Maybe I do know what I want.* His hands set firmly on my shoulders, and he bent to kiss the top of my head. "We'll tell them one way or another Saturday; don't fret over something this simple."

"You're right."

He walked away, and I continued uploading the pictures from the camera memory card to the hard drive on my laptop. After they finished, then I uploaded the pictures from our cell-phones to the hard drive.

****

Saturday was here before we knew it. I had everything ready to go for the presentation. Abby was helping me cook, or at least, I told her she was helping me. I let her get things from the refrigerator for me. She spent a lot of her time playing with her doll.

"How are my two favorite girls doing in here?" Jeff broke into my concentration with his deep, sultry voice.

"Good," Abby replied. She didn't look up from her doll. I looked up and smiled once Jeff's gaze met mine.

"And you, my love, how are you feeling?" His face softened, and a crooked smirk curled one side of his mouth up. *He is so fucking hot.*

"Perfectly ecstatic. I don't think I could possibly feel better or be happier than I am right now." My eyes lingered on his beautiful smile.

"I'm going to set up things downstairs."

"You don't want to be up here? You could help me cook." I winked at him before stirring the food bubbling on the stovetop.

"I think I'm better off downstairs right now. We have everything we need, but I'll make sure we have plenty of soda pop and water in the refrigerator so it's cold by the time our friends arrive. I also need to get the tables set up."

"You're right. We'll be eating down there anyway, and then head in to the movie theater to watch the slideshow."

"Exactly."

"Let me know if you need me to do anything or need any help."

"You, baby doll, will not be lifting or moving anything. Connor is coming by soon and he'll be helping."

"Fine. I'll be down, though, a little later. I need to get the crock pots set up on the counter."

The doorbell rang, and Jeff left the kitchen to answer it. It was Connor. Connor gave me my hug hello, then the two of them disappeared down the basement stairs.

I washed the five crock pots, filled them with the food to be kept warm, then took each of them down to the bar counter. The ribs, lasagna, and the sausage and peppers, would be kept warm in the chafing pans. Abby walked up and down the stairs behind me each trip.

Mom was bringing by two apple pies. Apple pie was my weakness. I could eat one whole pie all by myself. As I set the final pan in place, I could hear the faint sound of the doorbell. I ran up the stairs, Abby close behind me on my heels. We both walked to the front door, me gasping for air, Abby mocking me with her breathing. I couldn't help laughing as I opened the door.

"Oh my god, you're early." Jackie had arrived before anyone else, even before my mother. "What is the world coming to?" As she entered the house, Hunter walked in behind her.

"I figured I'd surprise you today." Jackie smiled and pushed past me.

"Hey Hunter, good to see you again." I gave him a quick hug.

"Hey beautiful, good to see you, too." Hunter was gorgeous. I was surprised he wasn't with someone when he arrived.

"Jeff and Connor are downstairs."

"I figured I'd come by early to see if you needed help with anything," Jackie said. "You didn't answer your phone."

"Yeah, it's buried in my purse. You can come keep me company, but I have everything done, for the most part."

"So how was Hawaii?"

"Freaking awesome," I sang out. Just the mention of the honeymoon had me flashing back.

"I hope you took a lot of pictures."

"We took a ton of pictures. We're going to show them later. You have to make a promise to yourself, Jackie, you have to go to Hawaii."

"Have to?"

"Absolutely, have to."

"I'll put it on my wish list."

"Put it on your must-do list, seriously."

We continued to talk and were joined by everyone else trickling in. Jeff, Connor, and Hunter all came upstairs to join the crowd that had formed in the kitchen. We were waiting for Mom and Jim to arrive before we all went downstairs.

I gasped in a deep breath as Jeff walked toward me. "What's wrong?" he whispered in my ear.

"I forgot to put out the plates and eating utensils downstairs." I felt so agitated and whispered into his chest, "Shit." I went to stand up, but he held me in place.

"You can thank Connor for doing that. Everything is set downstairs. We dug my two old folding tables out of the storage area and set them up, too." He leaned in and kissed my temple.

The doorbell rang and made me jump. "Relax, baby. I'll get it." Jeff walked to the front door. I was mesmerized by him. I wondered if I'd ever get tired of staring at him.

Never.

Abby ran to the door behind him and screamed when Jeff opened it. "Nana!"

"Hi, Abby. Hi, Jeff, good to see you." Mom's voice was warm. I watched as Jeff welcomed them in. He gave Mom a hug and shook Jim's hand.

We encouraged everyone to go downstairs, then told them to feel free to help themselves to the food. Jeff and Connor each had a drink in hand within minutes of going in the basement, and Jeff made Jim a drink, as well. I noticed Jeff and the guys had gathered together, while all of the women had gathered around me. Abby was perched on my hip. I was being bombarded with questions about the honeymoon, just as we had anticipated.

"We have a lot of pictures we're going to show you all on the movie theater screen in a bit. After we eat."

"I can't wait."

"Where all did you go?" Georgia asked.

"We spent three days on the Big Island, then we went to Kauai for three days and our last three days were in Maui. We went back to the big island for the final day before flying home."

"That sounds so amazing," Candace said.

"Yeah, it was." I sighed. "But Mom knows, she went to Hawaii for her honeymoon with Jim."

That was a great way to redirect some of the attention. I wasn't the only one who had been to Hawaii, and they had been to Oahu and Lanai. I let her tell them her stories while I got some food.

"I see your appetite is back; that's a good thing," Mandy said. She heaped some lasagna on her plate.

"Oh my gosh, Mandy. I ate like a freaking horse in Hawaii." I searched for Abby and saw she was still working on her food; her plate was sitting on one of the tables. She was having a good time wandering around talking to everyone.

"Do you think you guys will go back anytime soon?"

"Maybe in a couple years. I loved it, but I'd like to go to the Caribbean next trip."

"You'll like that."

"Hey, why didn't Creighton come with you today?"

"Creighton and I." She swallowed, "we are, um ... taking a break from each other right now."

"Oh, no! What happened?"

"It's a long story, for another day. I'm not talking about it now."

"Do you think you'll get back together?"

"Maybe, I don't know." She wiped her napkin at the corner of her eye to dab up the tear before it fell. "Maybe this is it."

"Oh, sweetie." I gave her a hug.

"Don't say anything; no one knows yet."

"My lips are sealed. I won't say anything."

"Today is your day; we can talk during the week."

 Jeff

I interrupted all the conversations and let everyone know that, when they were ready, we were set to show the pictures in the movie theater. Nikki grabbed Abby and wiped her fingers off. Then she made sure the lids were on all the dishes so the food would stay warm.

She was the last one to enter the movie theater. Abby was sitting next to Nikki's mom and Jim. I dimmed the lights, and we began showing the pictures. After I took a seat in the back, I pulled Nikki down onto my lap. Her arms snaked around my neck and her head laid on my shoulder. *God, I loved her touch.*

She had put the presentation together to show only one hundred of the over three hundred pictures we took. There was so much talking as the pictures changed. The helicopter aerial shots, waterfall, and volcano pictures garnered the most reaction.

The final slide displayed a blank screen. That caught me by surprise because I thought the slides were finished. Then a pair of pink booties flew in on the screen, followed by the word 'or' and then a pair of blue booties appeared. Everyone was really quiet.

Without warning, her mom gasped. Jackie stood up and turned to look at both of us. "Are you kidding?"

I helped Nikki stand so I could get up and turn on the lights. I pulled Nikki's hand into mine, then pulled her closer to me. I wrapped my arm around her shoulder, cleared my throat, and announced, "Yes, we're expecting a baby."

We all left the theater, and the basement was abuzz with questions about the baby. Everyone congratulated us both. They were all surprised to learn Nikki was almost four months along.

"Did you hear that, Abby? Mommy is going to have a new baby." Nikki's mom said. She seemed very disturbed by the announcement. I couldn't tell if it was because we had just gotten married or because we kept it from her.

Chapter 12

I convinced Mom to come with me to my next doctor's appointment. Jeff was going to be out of town, and I needed to understand what was bothering her now. Jeff and I both had noticed her agitation at the party.

I was lucky enough to get the first appointment of the day. I didn't want to miss much time from work, especially after my two-week vacation for the honeymoon and the few days off before the wedding.

After dropping Abby off at day care, I drove to Mom's house to pick her up and decided to just jump in feet first to get to the root of what was bugging her. She took a seat in the car and held her lips tightly pursed, as if she'd sucked on lemons all morning.

"Good morning, Mom."

"Good morning, dear." Her words were abrupt.

"What's wrong? Is something bothering you?"

"Oh, no, it's nothing."

Fucking lies. She thinks I don't know she's pissed about something? "No, Mom, I think something is bothering you. It was on Saturday, too. I could tell. I think we should talk about it."

"Well, if we must." She avoided looking at me and stared out the side window. I hated playing this game with her.

"Yes, we must."

"I'm hurt, that's all. And a little disappointed. I can't believe you felt you couldn't confide in me that you were pregnant."

"Mom, you know good and well if I had told you, you'd have had one more reason not to like Jeff."

"How long have you known?"

"Remember Christmas Eve, when I ended up in the hospital?"

She gasped and her head turned toward me. "So you thought it was better to lie to me than to tell me the truth about the baby?"

"Well, technically, I didn't lie to you. I wasn't the one that answered you, Jeff did." *Well, nice, I just threw my husband under the bus.* "We didn't want the pregnancy to overshadow the wedding, that's all."

"Do you think it's wise to have a baby so soon after getting married?"

"Wise or not, Mom, it's going to happen. I'd rather have waited, but things just happened. We didn't plan for this."

She didn't reply for quite a few minutes. "I surely hope you never tell the baby he or she was an accident."

I had to bite my tongue. I made the turn into the doctor's office and parked. "Mom, it's going to be okay."

"I hope, for your sake, it is. You two don't really even know each other that well, and now, you're having a baby." She turned her eyes away from me and just shook her head.

No sooner had I checked in, I was ushered back to the room right away. One of the beautiful things about that first appointment of the day, there are no good excuses why they can't see you on time. The nurse weighed me and took my blood pressure. I had gained eight pounds. I didn't think that was so terrible since I was over four months along and I still fit in my normal clothes.

When the doctor came in, he went over my last menstrual cycle, again. He asked how I was feeling and checked my lungs and heart – all the normal stuff. He told me his guesstimate was that I had conceived sometime between October nineteenth and the twenty-third. That explained a lot. It was in November that my dizziness and nausea had begun. I shuddered when I thought back to Thanksgiving and that disgusting smelling turkey. Then he told me my approximate due date was July twenty-seventh, but they'd get a better idea when I had the ultrasound.

When I finished and went to the receptionist, I made an appointment to get my ultrasound the next week and my regular appointment for the next month. Mom and I left and decided to stop to get coffee and a pastry from Starbucks. She continued with her relentless tirade.

"Why isn't Jeff going to these appointments with you?"

"He has to work. He can't just stop everything because I have a doctor's appointment. He'll be around when I get closer to my due date."

"I think it's very peculiar that he can't make arrangements to be by your side. It's his kid, too."

"He and I talked about this, Mom. I'm fine with things like they are."

"Well, I wouldn't be. Sky never would have let you go to an appointment without him."

"Sky didn't work consistently either," I snapped at her. I couldn't believe she was comparing the two. I was married to Jeff now. It didn't matter what Sky would or wouldn't do.

"I wasn't trying to upset you, sweetie." *Kind of too fucking late for that.* She took cheap shots at Jeff, which she knew would infuriate me, then said she didn't mean it.

"Let's change the subject then." I forced out between my clenched teeth. We switched to talking about Jim and his health. She told me they still had no idea what was going on with him. He had another round of tests coming up in a few weeks. We finished our coffee and pastry, then I took her back home before I drove in to work.

Jack had the week off, but I knew I'd have to talk to him next week. I had let his administrative assistant know about my doctor's appointment and my upcoming appointment the following week, but I'd have to let Jack know I was pregnant. I was looking forward to that conversation as much as I'd look forward to being run over by a truck.

"Nikki, we're going to the pizza joint. Do you want to join us?" Georgia asked.

"Are you kidding? I'm starving. Absolutely."

I thought it was going to be Candace, Georgia, and me, but Tristan and Robert joined us as well. We all met at the elevator, then walked over together. Almost all the questions were about either the honeymoon or my pregnancy. I regretted telling them I was getting my ultrasound the next week as soon as the words left my mouth. The questions focused on the preference of boy or girl and my speculation around what I thought Jeff wanted. I love them all, but they were giving me a headache. I had forgotten how crazy Candace and Georgia had been when I was pregnant with Abby. It was all coming back to me though.

Before we cleared our paper plates, Georgia made a comment about me finally eating instead of picking at my food. We finished and made our way back to the office.

It was tough getting back into the swing of things. The rest of the week, I struggled to concentrate on my work. The questions eventually ended, but I knew after the ultrasound they would ramp up to full speed again. I was counting down the days until Friday. I needed a break, and I was looking forward to going to Jeff's mom's house, my mother-in-law now. We still hadn't told her that I was pregnant.

****

Saturday morning, Sky and Hope came by early to pick up Abby. I had talked with Abby earlier in the week, and told her more about the baby, but I could tell she didn't seem to get it. She was young. When I told her the baby was in my tummy, she just looked at me. Sky and Hope were going to talk with her, too.

They were going to visit his mom for the weekend. *I hope that bitch treats Hope better than she treated me.* I wasn't really hopeful that she would; she was the epitome of evil in my book. I was so happy I didn't have to deal with her anymore.

After they left, I went back upstairs and climbed back in the bed. I was exhausted.

The caress down my bare arm was familiar; I could feel him. His fingers glided down my back, over my buttocks, then down the backside of my leg. I was paralyzed by his touch. He had me squirming, aching for more. But why couldn't I see him? I couldn't open my eyes, they felt like they had been glued shut.

I felt his warm breath near my ear-lobe. Was he trying to tell me something? I couldn't hear him. I could smell him. That wonderful smell of hotel soap and a hint of his spicy woodsy cologne. *Jesus, what if it wasn't him? What if someone broke in the house?*

I sprang up in the bed, gasping for my next breath as I looked around the room in a panic. I was blinking my eyes furiously as my heart beat so fast I thought it would burst out of my chest. I wiped the sweat from my forehead. Then I heard his snore, and I looked down before reaching over to touch the form lying next to me. I took in a deep breath and slowly exhaled. *It was him; he was home.*

I laid back down, and his arm reached across me, pulling my back into his chest. "You all right, baby?" he mumbled in my ear.

"Yeah, I am now."

I felt Jeff get out of the bed, and I rolled to look at the clock. I couldn't believe it was nearly one o'clock. The room darkening shades made it so easy to sleep.

I was lying on my side, facing the bathroom, when he walked out. "When do you want to go see your mom?"

"That can wait until later. Right now, I'd like my wife to let me know she appreciates me being home as much as I appreciate being here with her."

I sat up, grabbed his hand, and pulled him to me. "I'm very happy you're home."

Chapter 13

The visit with Jeff's mom went great. She was such a nice, caring woman. When we told her about the baby, she smiled and said she already knew. I had known that. I wasn't sure how she could tell though.

When Jeff had voiced his concern about the baby's health, his mom had replied to him letting him know he couldn't live in fear of things like that. I think Jeff and I both needed to hear her comforting words.

The rest of the weekend was perfect. Abby was brought back home just in time to see Jeff before he left for the week. When Sky, Hope and Jeff all left, Abby and I curled up and watched her favorite show, Sponge Bob, until she fell asleep.

That blaring alarm on Monday mornings completely sucks. I always feel like I didn't get enough sleep the night before.

I pulled a dress out of the closet to slip on for work. I tossed it on the bed, then made my way into the bathroom to take my shower. After getting ready, I went to get Abby. After getting her dressed, we made our way downstairs.

It didn't take us long to get out of the house and for me to drop her off before driving in to work. It had been nearly three weeks since I'd seen him. I had my one-on-one, and that was probably going to be as good a time as any to let him know about the baby. I entered the parking garage. It seemed more crowded than normal.

The elevator opened up, and I stepped off, walking down the hall as if I were walking the green mile. I made my way to my desk, put my purse in my drawer, and picked up my coffee cup. Just as I turned, I found myself face-to-face with Jack. "Wow, you startled me." I couldn't believe he walked up on me like that, not saying anything.

"Good morning, Nikki. I didn't mean to catch you by surprise. I figured I'd stop by to see if we needed to have our meeting today or if you'd rather move it to later in the week." He tugged at the waistband of his pants. "You know, since you've been off, I wasn't sure if we really needed to meet."

"I do have a couple of things to discuss with you today, if you have time."

"No problem at all. I'll get my coffee and be ready in a few minutes."

I held up my coffee mug. "I'm doing the same."

"Shall we, then?"

We walked down the hall, and Jack apologized again for not being able to attend the wedding. I assured him I understood that he had a prior commitment. I had completely forgotten he hadn't been there.

We met in his office, and he closed the door. "So how was the honeymoon?"

"It was great. Hawaii is beautiful. I hope to get back again soon."

"Did you guys do anything exciting?"

"We did a few things on each of the islands. We took a helicopter tour, did some hiking and sightseeing, we went on a dinner cruise, and a few other things. It was definitely somewhere I'd like to visit again."

"Well, congratulations, again."

"Thank you." I smoothed my dress across my lap. "I do have some other news, as well."

"Please don't tell me you're resigning."

"No, nothing like that. I'm expecting."

"Expecting?" He looked confused. "Oh, expecting a baby? Really?"

"Yep, I am. We are."

"When is your due date? Or don't you know that yet?"

"The doctor said July twenty-seventh. I have an ultrasound appointment tomorrow morning and they said they could give me a better idea then, if it was different."

"Well, keep me posted. I'll begin making plans for your replacement while you're out." He shifted some papers on his desk. "You will, um, be back, right?"

"I plan to be back, yes."

"Great to hear." He sat up straight and pushed his shoulders back. "Anything else we need to discuss?"

"No, that's it for me."

"And I don't have anything, so I guess we'll catch up again next week, if not before."

I stood and left, pulling the door closed behind me. I never stopped at my desk. I walked straight down to the break room to get another cup of coffee.

The rest of the day breezed by. I was happy to have the day end. After picking up Abby, I convinced her, with very little effort, we should eat at McDonald's for dinner. I was starving, and she loved their French fries. I'd also promised to let her spend about twenty minutes in the play area before we went home.

I had called Mandy earlier and she had agreed to meet me after work.

"Hey, there," Mandy said.

"Hey. How are you doing?" I stood to hug her.

"Eh." She shrugged her shoulders.

"So, tell me, what's going on with you and Creighton?"

"It's a long story, Nikki. You know, we've always kind of had a weird relationship."

"Yeah, but he loves you."

"I know. He said it several times, after I told him I thought we need time away from each other."

"Oh, no! You told him?"

"I had to. I began to feel … smothered. I love him, but I don't feel like I'm in love with him anymore. I miss him now that we are apart."

"You have to work on the relationship, Mandy. It's not easy. Maybe you and Creighton can date each other again."

"That seems strange. Date my husband."

"Why not? That was how you fell in love with him. Maybe it will help you fall in love with him all over again."

"Mommy!" Abby ran over and interrupted our conversation.

"Hey, Abby." Mandy smiled at her.

"Hi, Aunt Mandy."

Mandy looked at me and whispered, "And Creighton wants one of these." She nodded her head in Abby's direction.

"Oh, wow."

"Yeah, wow."

"I'm ready to go home Mommy."

Mandy stood up. "I'm not going to keep you, I need to leave anyway. Stay in touch, and I'll keep you posted on my situation."

"I'll definitely stay in touch." I picked up my purse and lifted Abby up onto my hip. We walked out to our cars together.

By the time we left to go home, I was so tired I could barely keep my eyes open. It was so weird how I could be wide awake one minute and ready to collapse like a narcoleptic the next. Maybe that was it, maybe I had narcolepsy now. *No, I'm being ridiculous, again.*

We walked through the door, and I suddenly felt wide awake. This pregnancy was so strange. I never went through this when I was carrying Abby. We sat up and watched Cartoon Network for a couple hours until Abby fell asleep in my arms. I got her in bed, then went back down to get my phone and make sure the doors were locked before retreating up to our room. Once there, I called Jeff and filled him in on the activities of the day, less the McDonald's dinner.

I woke in the morning excited and anxious. Today was the big day. I'd be getting the ultrasound. I would get the first glimpse of the baby.

Abby and I made pretty good time getting out of the house and to the day care center. Once I left, I called Mom to let her know I was on my way. I had to pee so badly, yet I was still drinking water. If they made me wait too long, I was sure to piss myself.

Mom and I arrived five minutes before my appointment and within minutes of checking in, I was called back. They were a little reluctant to let Mom accompany me, but at my insistence, they agreed. She sat on the opposite side of the technician.

"How far along did the doctor say you were?" The cold goop was shaken down in the bottle and squirted on my stomach.

"Four months."

"I can't believe you aren't showing yet. When I was four months, I was in maternity clothes and pretty big," the technician said. She stroked the wand across the goop to spread it across my lower belly.

"With my daughter, I was showing before three months."

"Oh, so this is your second pregnancy?"

"Yep, baby number two."

"Well, congratulations." The conversation ceased when she went back to watching the monitor. She moved the wand across my belly, digging into my stomach on occasion to take a picture.

I let out a small groan. I was pretty sure if she pressed in the right spot, I'd pee.

"Are you doing okay? Can you hang in there for just a few more minutes?"

"Yeah, I'm fine."

"I'll let you up to go to the bathroom in a little bit. I just need to capture a couple more shots."

She continued to probe and prod me with that wand, then removed it and wiped all the gel off my stomach. "All done; you can go to the bathroom. When you come back, we can talk."

I couldn't get off the table fast enough. After relieving my bladder, I returned and was directed to take a seat instead of climbing back on the table.

"Everything looks good; the baby seems to be developing fine."

"Could you tell if it was a boy or girl?"

"No, not yet. You can make a follow-up appointment when you get closer to six months, and we should be able to get some better pictures by then." She reached over to the table where the monitor was. "Speaking of pictures, I wanted to give you this one. It was such a perfect shot of the baby sucking his or her thumb."

I sat and stared at it. Emotions welled up in me and I could feel the prickly sting of tears. This was my baby, Jeff's baby, our baby. I couldn't wait for the day that I could hold this beautiful little bundle in my arms. I reached over and showed my mom. "Here you go, Mom, the first look at your newest grandson or granddaughter."

Mom took the film from my hands and sighed. As much as she may not care for Jeff, I knew she would love this baby every bit as much as all the others. There was no denying my mom's love for her grandchildren.

The technician continued, "You can call your doctor later today or tomorrow if you have any concerns or questions." She stood from her chair. "If you don't have any questions for me, I'll see you in a couple months. You can make an appointment with the receptionist out front now, if you want."

I stood. "Thank you."

Mom thanked her as we walked out the door.

Candace and Georgia must have sensed my presence when I got to work because it only took a few minutes after I got sat and logged on for them to show up at my desk.

"How'd it go?" Georgia asked.

"It went great. I need coffee desperately; want to walk down with me? I can show you the picture, too."

"Sure," Candace replied. She brandished her new mug.

I had the small picture in one hand and my coffee cup in the other as we walked down to the break room. Before getting my cup of coffee, I took a napkin and laid it out on the countertop, then set the picture on it and took a picture with my phone. With the click of a couple buttons and a short message, I sent the picture to Jeff.

"What's that?" Georgia was looking around Candace to see what I had.

"That's … wait. Is that the picture of the baby?" Candace asked.

"Yup. I just took a picture of it to send to Jeff."

"You know we want to see it."

We sat down at the table in the break area, and they passed the picture back and forth between each other.

"Do you know if it's a boy or girl yet?" Candace asked.

"No, not yet. The technician said I'd need another ultrasound in a couple months."

"Are you going to find out?" Georgia asked as she stared at the picture of the baby.

"Yeah, I am. I want to know."

"What if Jeff says he doesn't want to know and tells you not to find out?" Candace asked. Georgia passed the picture back to Candace.

"Ugh, I never thought of that. I don't know what I'll do if he says something like that." I took a sip of my coffee. "Maybe I'll find out and just not tell him." We laughed as the picture was handed back to me. "I better get back to my desk, though. I've had all this time off and now more with the baby. I don't need Jack getting pissy with me."

"Yeah, we need to get back to work, too. We'll see you later," Candace said.

Just before four thirty, I called the doctor's office and talked to his nurse. She told me pretty much the same thing the technician had said. The baby was developing just fine, the measurements were consistent with the estimated dates of conception, and the due date was still July twenty-seventh.

I couldn't quite put my finger on it, but something about the dates was unnerving.

Chapter 14

I sat up, jumping out of my sleep. My hands were shaking, and I was holding my breath. I couldn't see anything; the room was jet black.

"No!" I forced out. My breaths burned my lungs as they burst in and out of my mouth. Sweat was dripping from my hairline. I could only imagine every bit of color had drained from my face. I couldn't remember very much that had scared me this much before.

I'd had a dream that Sky was in the delivery room with me, Jeff was nowhere to be found, and the baby looked exactly like Sky. His mother was there, spewing her venom at me about how I had done it again. I had another baby to trap her son into coming back to me. Hope was there crying and being consoled by Sky's mom. And my mom stood in a corner just shaking her head in disgust, chanting how much I had disappointed her. She told me I had managed to ruin another marriage.

My body shook as I inhaled deeply, then exhaled. *Oh. My. God. That would be a total disaster.*

The only reason I could think of that I would have that dream was after I had talked to Jeff and was lying in the bed last night, it had all of a sudden hit me why the dates the doctor gave me were eating at me so much. My last known period was early in October. I definitely remembered Jeff and I having our conversation to come up with the wedding date on Saturday, October thirteenth. It was that next day we had the argument over the prenuptial agreement.

Then, the following Saturday, I had slept with Sky when I dropped off Abby. *I was so screwed. What if this baby really was Sky's?* I'd lose Jeff for sure if this wasn't his child. I'd lose Jeff if he ever found out I had slept with Sky.

I couldn't lose Jeff.

I couldn't live without him.

The thought of not having Jeff in my life made it nearly impossible to breathe.

I shook my head. My palms were clammy, and every muscle in my body was tight. I wasn't even tired any more. I had to figure something out. I needed to know, but paternity tests can't be done until the baby is born. *What was I thinking? I couldn't get a paternity test.* A paternity test was the quickest way to admit I'd been unfaithful. What a twisted mess.

How would I ever know? And when? I dropped my head, completely disgusted by myself. This wasn't going to affect just me; this would crush so many people.

I felt weak and sick.

It was four thirty-five in the morning, and I was wide awake, but I couldn't get up. I had to try to go back to sleep for at least another hour and a half. Then I'd be forced to get up for work.

I laid my head back down on the pillow and closed my eyes as I willed myself to go back to sleep. That dream was haunting my thoughts. I couldn't shake the thought of this baby looking just like Abby and Sky. The tears that lingered in my eyes slid down my face wetting my pillow case.

I pulled Jeff's pillow into my arms, holding it tight. My tears fell uncontrollably as I inhaled Jeff's scent.

The alarm clock scared the crap out of me when it went off a little while later. I rubbed my eyes and I quickly realized I was going to dread this day. I wanted nothing more than to lie back down and keep sleeping. At that moment, I asked myself, once again -- why was I still working? I loved my job. Plus, I loved not being dependent on anyone. I pressed the snooze bar, clutched Jeff's pillow tight to my chest, and pulled the sheet over my head. I never wanted to leave this spot.

The five minutes passed and the alarm blared at me, screaming for me to get up and get ready for work.

After I was dressed, I went and got Abby up. We slowly walked down the stairs, my mind racing.

My life was a conundrum.

I popped the Eggo waffle for Abby in the toaster and included one for myself. I didn't know why, because I wasn't hungry. When they popped up, I was so deep in thought, Abby called to me to let me know her food was done.

After she ate and we both were ready to go, we left the house so I could drop her off at the day care center. I heard one of the directors of the center talking, but for the life of me, I have absolutely no idea what she said.

The drive into work was done on auto-pilot. I couldn't tell you what roads I drove on to get to the office.

Luckily, I was a creature of habit and parked in the same general area every day or I wouldn't have been able to find my car after work.

I walked in the building and rode up the elevator with several other people. I moved back against the elevator wall and tried to shrink as low as possible. I didn't want to talk to anyone. I didn't want to be there. I had considered faking being sick so I could just go home.

****

I managed to keep a low profile and made it through the day. Eyebrows raised when I declined going to lunch. Instead, while they were gone, I raided the vending machine and ate two bags of wavy potato chips, a bag of Doritos, and a lemon pie. Not the best for me, but I knew Candace and Georgia would sense something was wrong if I spent too much time around them.

When I got to the car, I knew a trip to McDonald's was in order after I picked up Abby. I was starving.

We sat at a small table and ate our food while chatting about her day. She had it so easy. I envied her. I made her food, I washed her clothes, I read bedtime stories to her, and now, I was treating her to McDonald's. I missed being a kid.

"Can I go play, Mommy?"

"Sure, baby. Have fun. I'll tell you when it's time to leave."

She jumped up and took off running with a little boy on her heels as she let out a high-pitched squeal.

I watched her run off to the pit of plastic balls. I wished I could go back and change things in my past, but I couldn't. If I could change just one thing, I wished I could go back and change the weekend I slept with both Sky and Jeff. How could I face them? Somehow, some way, I had to figure that out, and fast. Jeff and I were going to Skype later that night, and I couldn't let him see concern on my face and ask me about it. I had to appear as if everything was normal.

"Excuse me, is that your daughter over there?" My eyes raised to see a younger man, probably a little younger than I, standing before me.

"Yes, she's mine." I flashed a toothy proud smile and turned my eyes to watch Abby laughing and tossing the balls in the air. I could see a cute little blond-haired boy in the pit of balls with her, doing the same.

"That's my son in with her. She's very pretty." I glanced up at the man. This guy was wearing a T-shirt and jeans. He was not much taller than I was, if even that tall. He had chunky sandals on. I detested those big, thick, bulky sandals on men. I had no idea why, I just did.

"Thank you. What a little cutie he is." I again returned my gaze to the kids. I didn't want this guy to get the wrong impression. But my attempt failed, and he sat in the seat that had once been occupied by Abby.

"My name is Bill. And you are?" His arm stretched across the table with his hand out for me to shake.

"I'm Nikki." I was very short with my reply, but I shook his hand.

"Ah, a very nice name. Nikki."

Where was this going? I wanted to tell him to scram, but not knowing if he was just being nice because our kids were playing or if he was trying to pick me up, I decided to bite my tongue and see if he would make a move.

"So, Nikki, are you dating anyone or married?" And there it was.

"Yes." I flashed my ring at him. "Happily married. A newlywed, in fact."

"Well, congratulations." The color of his cheeks became pink.

"Thank you." I didn't want to get engaged in a lengthy conversation about our personal lives. I wasn't interested in his marital status, but I gathered from his reaction he wasn't married. I was ready to get Abby and leave.

As if she read my mind, she tumbled out of the ball pit and walked over to me, hugging my arm. "I'm ready to go," she whispered to me, peeking around me to see the stranger sitting in her seat.

I smoothed her static-filled hair. "Okay, we can go." I bent to pick up my purse and stood, lifting her onto my hip before turning to Bill, who was now standing as well. "It was nice to meet you, Bill."

"It was nice to meet you, too." He smiled at Abby, but she buried her face in my shoulder.

I loved not having to cook when we got home. I took Abby up to take her bath, then we returned to the living room and watched Nickelodeon until she fell asleep. Her internal clock was set to have her fast asleep by eight thirty. A few minutes after I got her tucked in, I got my laptop and returned to my bedroom to talk with Jeff.

Chapter 15

I had decided I couldn't allow myself to be sucked into worrying about paternity right now, or at any time before I had this baby. I believed Jeff was the father. I had to believe Jeff was the father. He believed it, and Sky had not questioned it. Why would he? Neither one would know anything different until I was able to figure out how to determine anything that proved otherwise. And there was no way I wanted to wake out of my sleep or go through another mental breakdown about that concern again. The last time was worse than the night I had that nightmare.

I had a day where the thought of Sky being the father had completely consumed me. The morning had started out normal, like any other day. Then, about an hour into my work day, it spiraled to beyond horrible. I couldn't concentrate anymore at work. I tried desperately to shake the thought from my mind, but I couldn't. Everything I did somehow brought my thoughts back to that nightmare where the baby looked exactly like Sky. I had felt like I was having a nightmare while awake. I felt like everyone was staring at me, judging me because paternity wasn't one hundred percent known. I thought I was suffering from some form of psychosis.

The most horrifying thought of the whole episode was that I'd lost Jeff. I watched his back as he walked away from me. In my mind, I heard Hope laughing at me. She had called me a silly bitch and told me I'd never get Sky back, even if he was the father, and that I didn't deserve a man like Jeff.

By mid-day, when I was asked if I wanted to go to lunch, I broke down in tears. Candace and Georgia reluctantly went without me, at my insistence. I needed them away from me. I was going crazy and I had no intention of telling them what I had been thinking about. They felt a little better when I asked them to bring me back two slices of pizza.

By the time they returned, I was fine. Well, as fine as a possibly psychotic person can be. But I wasn't crying and I wasn't hallucinating anymore. When they asked me what happened and why I had been so upset, I blamed my breakdown on the stress of figuring out what to do for Jeff's birthday and my jacked-up hormones.

When Sky and Hope came to pick up Abby Friday night after Sky got off work, I scowled at Hope with renewed hate in my heart. After they left, I had to calm myself back down and convince myself that it wasn't real. The dream and that fucked up day weren't real.

Please, God, please, let Jeff be the father.

****

The next two months went by relatively fast. Hope had finally gotten moved in with Sky. A week before her move-in, Sky and I had made the changes to our agreement official for the visitation. He would get Abby every other weekend. If anything came up and he wanted her, he just needed to let me know. I thought it was best for us to keep some distance between us. Plus, I knew he'd want to spend time alone with Hope on weekends. It was a fair agreement for all of us, I thought. I was surprised he hadn't brought it up. He didn't seem to mind too much. The one who didn't understand the change the first couple of weekends was Abby, but she'd adjusted since then.

Each of my checkups went pretty much the same, still healthy as a horse and I was gaining weight like one. I had added on eight pounds one month and ten pounds the next. I knew my near nightly stops at McDonald's were to blame, but it gave me and Abby a chance to talk and eat without the hassle of me cooking and cleaning up. I had gained nearly thirty pounds so far. Way more than I would have guessed. I had hoped to only have gained thirty pounds during the entire pregnancy. *So much for that*.

I had my appointment the next day to get my ultrasound. Jeff had planned to be there for it, but Sandy was sick, and they needed Jeff to cover for him. That sucked. I really had hoped he could have been by my side when the doctor told us whether we were having a boy or a girl. Mom was going to go with me now.

She was busting at the seams to find out what her new grand baby would be.

I had the third appointment of the morning. With any luck at all, I would be seen close to my scheduled time.

Jeff told me to call him as soon as I left the doctor's office. He was in a meeting all morning, but said he would take my call no matter what.

I woke in the morning earlier than my alarm was set to go off. I was so excited. I hoped the doctors said I was having a boy. I'd have a perfect family if Jeff said no to more children. Plus, the idea of a mini-Jeff tearing around the house would be awesome. I had dreamed of a handsome little boy, with dark hair and those dreamy eyes, on more than one occasion. He would be tall, like his dad, taller than the other kids his age, and much stronger, too.

I took a shower and got dressed. I hated maternity clothes. I couldn't wait to fit back into my old clothes that had been packed up to make room for my new wardrobe.

My phone rang while I was combing my hair, startling me. I looked at the caller ID before answering.

I was so thrilled to see Jeff calling me. My heart lurched as I answered. "Hey, baby."

"How's my sweet thing doing this morning?"

I blushed. "I'm doing fine. The only thing that would be better would be having you here with me."

"I wish I were there, too. I just wanted to tell you how much I love you. I can't wait to hear the news."

"I love you, too. And I'll call as soon as I can."

"Perfect. I won't hold you, I know you have to get Abby ready. I'll talk to you soon. Give her a kiss for me."

"Okay, baby. I will. Bye." I hung up and clutched my phone to my chest.

I worked to get Abby up and ready so we could get moving. After dropping her off at the day care, I drove over to Mom's house, where she greeted me with a cup of coffee. We sat and watched some of the morning news program with Jim. After I finished my coffee, I drank a glass of water, then we said goodbye to him and left.

"Are you feeling okay? You look like you're gaining a pretty good amount of weight." Mom sounded like a combination of amused and appalled. She had commented throughout my pregnancy with Abby that she didn't think I was eating enough. She was always offering to bring food over to us and invited us to dinner on the weekends. Sky and I went, not because we didn't have food, but we both thought if she was going to cook, why not take advantage of her generosity.

"I'm holding a lot of water today." I laughed at my terrible joke. *I better watch laughing too hard; I might pee myself.* "I feel fine. And, yeah, my weight." I rubbed my hand across my tummy. "I just hope he or she is a big baby, because I'm really packing it on this time."

"Are you watching what you eat or are you eating everything in sight?" Ugh! I couldn't tell her my after work ritual; she would chastise me for sure.

"I'm trying to watch what I eat, but I take Abby to McDonald's every now and then on our way home. It's so much harder this time."

"You know you haven't even gotten to the months that you'll gain the most. You have two and a half more months to go."

"I know, I know. Please, don't remind me."

"As long as the baby is healthy, that's what matters. If you're eating everything in sight, there's bound to be enough nutritional value to share with my grandbaby." She chuckled. She actually sat there and laughed as if that was a joke.

I'm getting fat as fuck and she's laughing at me.

"I guess I'll just have to work extra hard to get it off."

"You're still young; you shouldn't have any problem. And, honey, try to stay away from McDonald's."

Ugh! I really didn't need a lecture on weight right now. I couldn't go on a diet, and I was only going to get bigger. Not only that, there were only two more weeks until Jeff's company picnic -- more food. I drank the last couple of gulps from my water bottle.

I turned into the parking lot and found a spot somewhat close to the door. We walked through the double doors and down the hallway to the office. After checking in, we sat and flipped through the pages of the magazines, anxiously waiting to be called back. I checked the clock -- shit, it was twenty minutes past my appointment time, *and I really needed to pee.*

"Nikki Carrington." I grabbed Mom's arm and pulled her up when I stood. I wasn't sure how long I'd be able to last before my bladder exploded. The nurse smiled at me as I waddled over toward her. *Who the hell waddles at six and a half months pregnant?* If anyone commented on it, I'd lie and tell them I hurt my back.

We made our way back to the small room full of equipment. The radiologist asked me the standard questions before telling me to remove my shirt, put on the gown, and lie down on the table.

After I had assumed the position, she shook the bottle of cold gel and squeezed it onto my stomach. "I'll go as quickly as I can. I know you're probably pretty uncomfortable."

You think? "I'm sure I'll be okay for a few minutes."

She began prodding and pushing that wand into my abdomen right around my bladder. I inhaled deep, and she pressed in and held the wand tight as she clicked the keyboard buttons. If she continued to press on my belly like that, I was going to piss myself for sure. She moved the wand around toward the side of my belly and clicked a few pictures from that angle.

She pressed down from the top of my belly and kept clicking the keys.

"You want to know the sex of your baby, correct?"

"Yes, we do."

"As soon as I get a perfect view, I'll take a picture for you." She clicked a few more keys on the keyboard. "I have a couple more angles to capture, then we'll be all done. How are you doing?"

"Barely hanging in there."

"Just a couple more seconds, I promise." She moved the wand in slow motion across my stomach, and I didn't think I could take it anymore. "All done. I'll get some of this gel off of you, then you can go to the restroom."

She pulled out a towel and wiped across my stomach once before I knew I had to get up. "That's good, I have to go, bad, right now." She helped me sit up, and I walked as fast as I could to get across the room and into the bathroom.

When I walked out, I breathed many sighs of relief. It had never felt so good to pee.

"Come on over and have a seat. I have a picture for you."

I almost came out of my skin. I was going to find out. And I had a picture so I could show Jeff our baby. I sat next to Mom and crossed my legs at my ankles.

"This picture is for you." She handed me the small square of film. "And you're having a boy; congratulations."

A boy.

A son.

Our son.

My eyes welled up and, as hard as I had tried not to allow it, a tear slid down my cheek.

Chapter 16

"It's a boy, baby! We're going to have a son!" I screamed into the phone. I didn't mean to scream, but when I heard him answer the phone, my emotions balled up in my throat and made it difficult to talk. I fought back most of the tears, but not all. I could hear him fighting to control his own emotions on the other end of the phone. I wanted to hold him. I wanted to see him.

"Oh my god! Really? A boy!" His voice cracked a little. "Baby, I'm so happy. I love you so much."

"I love you, too."

"I have to go, but I'm so happy you called. I'll call you later this evening."

"Okay, bye."

Mom was driving, which was a good thing for me.

"So I take it he's pretty happy?" Mom laughed as she reached out and rubbed her hand down my arm.

"Yeah, he is." I sighed. "You know, I didn't think he would warm up to having a baby as quickly as he did."

"Why would you say that? Why wouldn't he?"

I wanted to slap myself. I didn't mean to say that, especially not to my mom. "Well, he just wasn't sure if he'd want kids, but that was when we had first begun dating. We didn't really talk about it too much again after that."

"I'm sure his mother will be happy to know she's going to have a grandson."

"Yeah, I'm sure she will. She was happy just to hear she was going to be a grandmother." I shifted in my seat and turned slightly toward my mom. "How do you feel, Mom? Are you happy?"

"Sweetie, I'm happy as long as you are. I only want you to be happy." She looked at me, then turned her gaze back to the road. "Maybe I was wrong about Jeff. He seems to be a wonderful husband. He's not a lost soul anymore."

As soon as Mom made that statement, I remembered back to the day we were in the park. Jim, her, and I were there together, and she had told me there was a lost soul out there, and when he found me, he wouldn't be lost anymore. I leaned my head back on the headrest and smiled; a warmth rushed through my body as I wrapped my arms around my stomach, hugging my bundle of joy.

My son.

Our son.

Jeff

I sat in the conference room, not focusing on work. I saw their mouths moving, but not one word they were saying was registering in my brain. I tried like hell to concentrate, but I kept finding myself looking down at my cell-phone on the table off to the side of my notepad. At least I had told them I was expecting an urgent phone call and I'd have to take it.

My heart raced when my phone rang and Nikki's name displayed on my phone. I took in a deep breath, picked up my phone, excused myself, and walked quickly out of the conference room.

"Hey, Nikki." I couldn't tell if I had cleared the doorway or not and thought it would be better to use her name since I was at a client site.

"It's a boy, baby! We're going to have a son!" she screamed into my ear.

I closed my eyes as I stood against the wall by the elevator, out of sight. I could feel tears welling up behind my eyelids. My heart was beating so hard I could feel the pounding radiating through every inch of my body.

"Oh my god! Really? A boy!" I opened my eyes, took in a deep breath, and then sighed, trying to suppress the need to jump up and down while I screamed at the top of my lungs, *Fuck yeah, motherfuckers! We're having a boy!* "Baby, I'm so happy. I love you so much."

"I love you, too." I knew her voice well enough, and I knew she was crying. I was on the brink of losing my shit, too. God, I wished I was there to wrap her in my arms, just to hold her close to me. We could shed tears of joy together. I couldn't even explain the feeling that was running through me.

"I have to go, but I'm so happy you called. I'll call you later this evening."

"Okay, bye."

I wanted to tell the world; I wanted to shout to everyone. I wanted to dance around like a madman. I stood there for another couple of seconds before I walked back down the hall to the conference room. My steps were slow, hesitant. I wanted to turn on my heels and run the fuck out of there, drive to the airport and fly home, where I belonged. But I had to finish this. If we could get almost everything taken care of today, I could leave tonight. Blake could handle the rest, without me.

I had gathered myself pretty good as I reached for the door handle to enter the conference room.

"I apologize for that, but I had to take that call." I couldn't stop smiling.

"No worries; we hope everything is okay."

"Everything is great." I sighed. "Everything is perfect." I hadn't realized how wide my smile had grown or how utterly foolish I must have appeared to them all until I looked up and saw everyone staring at me with varying expressions of confusion. Even Blake. She looked at me with her lopsided smile, and eyes that wanted to know what was going on.

"So where were we?" I spoke up to get everyone's attention back onto the discussion we had started. I was on a mission to get this wrapped up, or as close to wrapped up as possible, by five o'clock.

We continued our discussions. We took a half hour break for lunch, then we got right back on-topic. I really hated these on-the-fly problem-solving meetings. If they knew there were problems, they should have said something. I could have had someone, anyone else, come with me besides Blake. Someone more technical. I'd have preferred that anyway. Maybe that was why Sandy was coming out originally; he was far more technical than Blake.

By the time we ended our meeting, the clients were happy. Well, almost happy, but Blake could finish things up the next day. I called my manager and told him how things were progressing and told him I wanted to leave that night instead of the next night. Once I explained why, he congratulated me, told me to get out of there, and to kiss Nikki for him. *I sure as shit planned to kiss her, but not for him.* Maybe before the night was over, I'd give her a little peck on the cheek from him. I hung back in the conference room and called the travel agent and told her to get my flight changed. Now I just had to wait for the text message with the revised itinerary.

When we got back to the hotel, I told Blake I was leaving. That didn't sit too well, but I really didn't give a damn. She tried to pretend like she wasn't sure she could get things wrapped up without me. I had dealt with that excuse from her before. The hard part was done. She had very little to finish, and there was no way I was hanging around to do that when she was more than capable of handling it.

I rushed up to my room and packed up all my shit in record-breaking time. I sat on the edge of the perfectly made bed, with one arm resting on my suitcase while tapping my foot. Just then I realized, I hadn't changed my clothes. I still had my suit on.

My phone lit up like a Christmas tree with the text saying my flight was leaving in two hours. Barely time to get to the airport and through security.

Fuck it. I hated flying in a suit, but I wasn't changing. I just wanted to go home and see my baby doll. There was no way I was missing that flight.

From the time I left the hotel in that cab, to the time I pulled up in my driveway, everything seemed to be moving in slow motion. But I was finally home. I jumped out of the car and ran to the front door, unlocked it, and stepped into a dark house. I kicked off my shoes and walked up the back stairs quietly so I didn't wake Nikki or Abby.

I opened the bedroom door and closed it behind me. Taking off that suit was long fucking overdue. I stripped down butt naked and walked over to the bed, sliding in under the sheets.

"Jeff?"

"Yeah, baby, it's me. Go back to sleep."

I curled my body around hers, snaking my arm around her round belly, holding her and my son tight to me. My son. I inhaled a deep whiff of her scent. I loved her smell, no body spray. Just that clean freshly showered smell topped off with cocoa butter body lotion. I felt her sink her back against my chest and I knew -- our life was perfect.

Chapter 17

I had come to hate the size of my body. Nothing I put on was flattering. Two weeks had gone by, and I felt like I was the size of a house. My whole body was so big for being seven months pregnant; bigger than when I was pregnant with Abby. I felt as miserable and fat as that reflection that stared back at me in the mirror looked.

"Babe, come on," Jeff hollered at me from downstairs.

I was dragging my feet on purpose. I didn't want to go. That was the bottom line. "I'll be down in a couple of minutes," I hollered back down as I jerked a yellow sun-dress out of the closet from its hanger and slowly drug it on over my head. It looked like a ten-man life raft draped over my shoulders. I looked hideous.

I went in the bathroom and saturated myself in my Be Enchanted body spray. I didn't know why. Habit, probably. Or maybe I just wanted to at least have one thing positive going for myself. I slid on my yellow slide-on sandals with the flower embellishment that I couldn't even see anymore, then headed downstairs to go to this godforsaken picnic.

"You look beautiful, baby."

Fuck off. Don't patronize me. "Thanks. I feel like a whale."

"I hate when you do that. Don't put yourself down." He walked over and wrapped his arms around my huge body. "At least you don't smell like one. You really do love torturing me with that smell, don't you?"

"What do you mean?"

"You know damn well what I mean." He pulled my hand down to feel his growing bulge. "I should take you upstairs and finish what *you* just started."

"I thought you were in a hurry to leave?" *How the hell is he even thinking of sex? Jeez, does he see me?*

"I think if we're a little late, no one will notice." He pulled me in tighter and bent down; his lips grazed mine, his tongue swiped between my lips, and his hands began manipulating the dress to raise it.

I broke our kiss. "Let's wait until we get back." I had on my huge, pregnant, granny panties that I thought would be a total mood killer. Somewhere between last month and this month, I had blown up like Violet from *Willy Wonka and the Chocolate Factory*.

"If that's what you want, then fine, I'll wait. I don't like it, but I'll honor your wish." He adjusted his cock, moving it around, while I pulled my dress back down and made sure it was on straight.

"We can go if you're ready." He picked up his keys off the hook of the key hanger by the door. I may not have had any of my furniture in the house, but I was finding small ways to add my touch.

I picked up my purse, made sure my cell phone was in it, and let him know I was ready.

The drive was quiet. I couldn't help but think how bitchy it had been to lead him on then shut him down. I knew good and well what that spray would do to him. I had done the same thing a few times in the past couple months. I just looked fucked up, and I felt anything but attractive. My feet always swelled in the evenings, and I was so tired. I enjoyed sex, when we eventually got to it. The problem was getting there. Maybe if I didn't resemble May Belle the cow, I'd have felt different.

I snapped out of my self-loathing when Jeff turned into the driveway of a beautiful chalet home. Once he stopped the car and turned it off, he leaned over to me, held me by my nape, and pulled me to him, our mouths crashing together. When he released me, he stared into my eyes. "Later baby, that pussy will belong to me. I won't take no for an answer. I need to feel you. Tell me you want me, too."

"Of course I do. I'm looking forward to it." *I really wasn't*, but I knew I couldn't deny him again. I didn't even have Abby to use as an excuse.

He walked around and helped me out of the car, then, holding my hand, we walked up to the front door and he pressed the doorbell.

In just a couple seconds, the door opened. My mouth dropped. *What in the motherfucking fuck?* It was *her*.

"Jeff." This stunning woman, with a perfect, tight body sang out my husband's name as she practically jumped out of the doorway at him. She slithered her arms around his neck in a way-too-tight embrace. She stepped back and took me in, and her eyes uncomfortably roamed my expansive figure. "And you must be Nikki. It's nice to meet you." Her voice was cold when she spoke to me. I hated her.

I had no idea who she was, but I didn't like the hug and didn't like her eye-balling me like that. I tried very hard not to let it show on my face. I plastered on a strained smile and extended my hand to shake hers. *I wanted to rip this bitch's arm out of its socket.*

Jeff placed his hand at the small of my back. "Baby, this is Blake."

Hold the God damn phone! What the fuck did he just say? This is **Blake***? Blake is a female?* My heart-beat sped up. I felt so heated, I thought I was going to pass out. I know my reaction had to have shown on my face. She took a step back, and Jeff stepped closer to me, wrapping his arm around my back.

Jesus fucking Christ. I rubbed my cheek with my right hand as I inhaled deeply. I wasn't going to cause a scene, but all

I could think was, *What in the actual fuck?* I forced my words through clenched teeth trying to hide my seething. "It's nice to meet you, Blake." We shook with limp hands. "Do you have any water? My throat is really dry." *Can you drown a bitch in a glass of water? I'll bet I could right now.*

I remembered her being in Jeff's house for his party when he proposed. I distinctly remembered the claim of an eyelash in her eye when she was in the kitchen and she asked to see my ring. But what was gnawing at my insides right here, right now, were the many times Jeff was out of town, rushing me off the phone because he and Blake were going to get something to eat or going out with clients. My heart plummeted into my stomach. *Blake and I, Blake and I ...*

Now I saw Blake was a beautiful, tall woman with piercing blue eyes. Not a man, as I had thought. And her eyes had lit up like a fucking Christmas tree when she saw Jeff at her front door. The sight of him made her come to life. The same eyes that dulled when she looked at me.

Fat, pregnant me.

"Sure, come in the kitchen. We have everything." She turned on her heels.

Before I took my first step, Jeff had his arm around my neck, had kissed my left cheek, and asked, "Are you all right?"

Are you kidding me? Are you fucking kidding me? Do I fucking look all right? "We'll talk later. But the short answer is no. No, I'm not fucking all right." I hissed as quietly as I could. I yanked my way out of his hold and waddled in the direction Blake had disappeared.

Once in the kitchen, she handed me a bottle of water, then motioned to a man who was clearly involved in a conversation. He excused himself and joined us.

"Jeff and Nikki, this is my husband, Jason. Well, Jeff, you already know him."

This couldn't be happening. This just fucking couldn't be happening. This Jason couldn't possibly be Jack's brother. What were the odds? Jack had told me that his brother worked at the same company as Jeff.

"It's nice to meet you." I extended my hand to his.

Jeff stood in his alpha stance, feet wide and arms folded across his chest. *Why was he posturing?* "Jase." Maybe I had jumped to conclusions that this might be Jack's brother.

Without warning, arms wrapped around me from behind. "Hey, beautiful." It was Connor. He turned me to face him, and I had to do everything in my power to fight back the tears that wanted to fall. "You look more and more stunning every time I see you, Nikki."

"Thanks. You don't have to lie to me, Connor." I chuckled, in hopes my fake laugh would hold my tears at bay.

"I'm not lying, Nikki." Connor had a look of pure innocence on his face.

"I told her the same thing before we left home." Jeff winked at me.

I squinted my eyes and shot Jeff the most evil look I could force without bursting into tears. My eyes dropped to the floor. "Well, thank you." I decided to drop it, for now. "Both of you." Continuing to discuss my looks standing in front of Blake was going to make me unravel. She was perfect, and I was far from it. Plus, nearly everyone here worked with Jeff, I had to keep control.

"Come outside, Nikki, I'll introduce you to some of the other people you haven't met, yet." Jeff clasped my hand in his and gave me a slight tug, pulling me along.

I looked over my shoulder at Connor. "I'll see you in a bit."

He smiled at me. My mind raced back to the day of the party, when Jeff had proposed. The day I saw Blake for the first time but never knew who she was. Why had Connor whisked her into the kitchen that day, as if he was trying to keep her away from me?

Jeff introduced me to several people who were out in the yard laughing and having a good time. They all spoke to me as if they had known me for years. Everyone was so nice. I couldn't help but notice the food they had on their plates, too.

We walked back toward the grill, and the fury in me began to rise when I watched Blake strut her gorgeous body out the sliding glass doors with the tongs in one hand and a pan in the other. I couldn't help but wish that she'd fall.

I didn't need any more food.

Ever.

"Shit." I stumbled over something as we walked across the lawn. My big toe on my left foot was throbbing.

"Are you okay?" Jeff stopped, staring into my eyes.

"I just tripped, I'm fine. Stop fussing over me."

"What the hell is bothering you?"

I looked around and saw no one was within earshot, but refused to say anything while here. "I'm fine; leave it alone."

He shook his head. His arms pulled me to him. He told me he loved me and his mouth came down on mine. For the first time ever, my body didn't react to his touch. He released me from his embrace. "You're my wife. If something's wrong, I want to know. I fucking need to know."

"Tell me what's going on with my toe. I can't see it." A single tear fell down my cheek. His hand wiped it away before he glanced down and gave me the answer.

"Come back to the house. It's cut and bleeding a little."

My world was falling apart. First I met this perfect bitch Blake, who I thought was a man, then Jack's brother was here, married to Blake, and now I had damn near ripped my toe from my foot. What the fuck else was going to go wrong today?

We walked into the house, and Jeff asked Jason for a Band-Aid and a wet paper towel. He sought out an empty chair and instructed me to sit down while he walked off, following Jason. No sooner had my ass hit the seat, than Blake surfaced. "What happened, sweetie?"

Don't fucking call me sweetie! My blood boiled. "I tripped in the yard."

"You need some peroxide. I'll be right back." Within seconds, she returned carrying the familiar brown bottle and a couple of cotton balls. She handed them to me. "Here you go; let me know if you need anything else."

What the fuck was I supposed to do with this? I could barely see my feet, let alone reach them. I sat in the chair and held the bottle and cotton balls, shaking my head in disbelief. What a disastrous day this was turning out to be.

Jeff returned with a Band-Aid and a paper towel in his hand. He knelt down in front of me before he took the peroxide and cotton balls out of my hands. After cleaning my toe off, he pulled the Band-Aid on snugly, then slid my flip-flop back on my foot.

"Good as new, Cinderella." He leaned in and kissed my forehead. "I'll be right back. I'm just going to go wash my hands."

I sat and talked to Sandy and his wife while Jeff was in the bathroom. When the two of them left me sitting alone, I went to find Jeff. I needed to go to the bathroom, and he had been gone for a lot longer than it would have taken him to pee and wash his hands. I walked back to the bathroom and could hear his voice, low, barely audible. I sneaked down the hall and peered into a room where the door had been nearly closed. I managed to see Jeff and Blake standing inches from each other.

Jeff's hand was resting on her arm. She looked sad, and the conversation appeared to be tense. She moved her hand up to his face and stroked down his bearded chin. My blood began to boil. He reached up and put his hand over hers. I wished I could hear what they were saying.

My stomach lurched. I turned and retreated, ducking into the bathroom, where I stared at myself in the mirror.

Fatty McFat stared back at me.

The tears trickled uncontrollably. I shook my head. Why would he bring me here? I sat on the closed toilet. I sobbed and wiped at my river of tears, but it did nothing to stop them.

"Nikki, baby." I could hear Jeff's muffled voice, but I didn't want to see him. I wanted to leave. "Nikki, let me in."

"I'll be out in a minute." I couldn't guarantee that. I had to pee and regain my composure. I could take care of going to the bathroom, but getting myself together, I didn't know if that could be achieved.

A few minutes later I walked out of the bathroom with a crooked smile on my face, hoping my pain wasn't visible to onlookers. Fortunately, there was only Jeff and one other person standing outside the bathroom door. His eyes were narrowed. He stood rubbing the back of his neck, and his jaw was clenched tight. He pulled me into him and kissed me. He release me and gasped. "Baby."

"I'm fine."

"Come on, we're leaving." His voice was low and strained, while he tapped his fingers on the moulding around the door.

Jeff ran his fingers through his hair as he said his good-byes, then held my hand and pulled me behind him.

We got in the car, and as he backed out of the driveway, he glared at me. "I'm trying really hard right now not to say something I'll regret, Nikki."

I turned my back partially to Jeff and stared out the window. *He had a lot of nerve talking to me like that.* So many things were racing in my mind. We rode in silence for several minutes. My stomach ached. A cramping ache that made my stomach tight. I hadn't eaten anything there, so I knew it wasn't food poisoning. After a few more minutes of silence, I couldn't take it any longer.

"Why, Jeff?" I sighed. Before he could get one word out, I continued. "Why would you take me over there?"

"Last I checked, you were my damned wife. It's an annual department picnic, and this year, I wanted to have you on my arm. Is that too hard for you to understand?" He slammed his fist on the steering wheel. "What the fuck is wrong with you, anyway? What did I do wrong?"

"Why was she hanging all over you?"

"What?" His head snapped in my direction. His eyes were dark and ominous. "Man, you have some serious fucking problems. You're really pissing me off today. If you weren't my wife, I swear to God, I'd put your ass out on the side of the fucking road. I don't have time for your jealous, insecure bullshit."

I turned my head back toward the window as tears jetted down my face. I knew what I had seen. Yeah, I might have been insecure, but there was no fucking way he could have convinced me that there hadn't been or wasn't something between them. My heart was destroyed.

Jeff

Why did I just say that to her?

Fuck!

There's no way I'd put her out on the side of the road. Jesus, she must think I'm a complete asshole right now.

She'd been testing my patience all day, though. She had no idea how much I hate hearing her talk about herself. She's pregnant, and the most beautiful woman in the world to me. She's carrying my baby, my son. A son I'd never be having if it weren't for her being part of my life.

And now this shit with Blake? I saw it in her eyes immediately. She doesn't even know her and she wanted to rip her throat out. When I went to get the Band-Aid and Connor said he noticed it, I knew other people had to have seen it, too.

Then Blake cornered me after I washed my hands. Fucking crazy bitch had the nerve to ask if I'd recommend she not be transferred. *No dice. I'm the one who made the request to have her transferred away from me.* I knew her working with me was trouble, but I had no say so in her getting that job. But now, with this promotion, I had more input and I let my manager know she'd be better suited for another position.

But Blake wasn't my problem, Nikki was. I had to find a way to make this right, and quick. I flipped through a couple CDs, then slid one in the player and turned the volume up. I knew she listened to the words of songs, so I had to find the right one to say what I wanted her to hear. Who knew I'd actually find a woman like me, someone who listens to lyrics.

I clicked to the track I wanted her to hear. I chuckled at the memory of when Nikki asked how far back my music collection dated. *Well, baby, I'm going way back, now.*

Seals and Croft was perfect. Diamond girl, she was my diamond girl. *For you, baby doll, you sure do shine... you're my Diamond Girl ... You've made me happier than you'll ever know.*

The song played, and her eyes remained fixed out the passenger's window. *Maybe she wasn't listening.* I reached my hand over and placed it on top of hers. "Nikki, I'm sorry." She turned and looked at me with puffy red eyes, then turned her eyes down at our hands. My chest ached, and there was a knot in my gut. "Will you forgive me for being an ass?"

She nodded her head, then turned and looked out the window again.

"Are you hungry? We didn't eat anything."

"Do I look like I need to eat?"

"Baby, you're pregnant, not fat. Please stop berating yourself."

She sat in silence. I was starving, so I wasn't in a rush to go home. She didn't seem to be in the mood to cook, and I sure as fuck wasn't going to.

"What do you say we go get something to eat?"

"Fine."

I knew that short answer *fine* all too well. It wasn't okay, not yet. I saw a sign for Wendy's and pulled into their parking lot. I got out of the car and went to her door and helped her out, then pulled her into my arms. I put my hand under her chin, and her eyes met mine. "Nikki, baby, I love you. Only you. There is no one else in this world for me. Do you understand that?"

She nodded as tears rolled down her cheeks. I pulled her in tight to me. *Why can't she see how much I love her?*

Chapter 18

Two weeks had passed since going to *her* house for the picnic, and my frustration and irritation were not waning. I had hoped I'd find a way to let it go, but the more I thought about it all, the angrier I got.

Hearing Jeff tell me it was nothing didn't do much to calm my suspicions. My thoughts flashed back to all the times he rushed me off the phone to go to dinner or attend a meeting with Blake. Me, foolishly, and unknowingly, telling him to not make her wait, *but I thought Blake was a* him *at the time. Blake, Blake, Blake* … over and over in my mind.

Why didn't he tell me? Why did he keep it a secret that Blake was a she? And now that I know, what do I do? What *do* I know?

So much really bothered me, especially seeing them in that room with the door barely open. Her with her paws on him, like he was her man to touch. And why didn't he tell her to take her hands off him?

I couldn't stand it any longer. I had to go talk to my mom now that she was back from her vacation. She would help ground me, and I desperately needed that right now. My mind was running wild.

After I called Mom and made sure she had time, I gathered Abby and went to pay her a visit that was two week overdue.

"Nikki, it's good to see you. Come on in, your mom's in the kitchen."

"Thanks Jim."

"How's married life treating you?"

"Things are good. I'll be happy when I have this baby, though."

He chuckled. "I'm sure you will."

We walked into the kitchen where Mom was washing all of two plates and two forks. "Hi Mom."

"Hi, sweetie, how are you? Have you been feeling okay?"

"Yeah, I'm good."

Jim seemed eager to get out of the kitchen. "I'll let you two talk, I'm heading back in to finish watching my show."

After he left the kitchen, my mom began her interrogation. "So what brings you over today?"

"Something's been on my mind for the past couple weeks and it's starting to drive me crazy."

"Tell me what's going on." Mom stopped washing dishes and leaned down to Abby. 'Hey, baby girl, can Nana get you anything to drink?"

Abby nodded her head and replied, "Juice."

"Ask the right way, Abby." I had to correct her. I didn't want her thinking she could start barking commands at people or go back to talking like a baby.

"Can I have juice, Nana? Please?"

"Why, of course you can, angel."

Mom got Abby her juice and she went in to watch TV with Jim.

"So what's got you so riled up?"

"Okay, so, on Memorial Day we went to a picnic with Jeff's co-workers, and I met another person he works with. Someone he's traveled with quite a bit, but I never met before. I thought all along the person was a man because of the name, but it turns out it was a female. Well, she still is a female."

"Darling, you had to have known deep down that Jeff works with both men and women. Of course he would have female co-workers."

"Yeah, I know. I get that." I huffed. "But when I saw her, she latched onto his neck like his long lost girlfriend."

"He's married to you. Did he seem to make you feel like he was happy about or welcoming of her clinging?"

"No, he didn't act like that. And he did wrap his arm around me when he introduced me to Blake."

"What was her name?"

"Blake."

"Blake?" I noticed that familiar look on my mom's face. That look that said she knew something. The hairs raised on the back of my neck as an eerie feeling washed over me.

"Yeah, Blake. And something about her just rubbed me the wrong way."

"Did you talk to Jeff about it?"

"Yeah, after we argued on the way home and he threatened to put me out on the side of the road. He basically told me I was nuts, that there was nothing for me to worry about." I looked at mom's face and swallowed hard. "You know something, don't you? I can see it on your face."

"Honey, I don't want to upset you any more than you already are."

"Mom, just tell me. What is it?" I could feel my throat beginning to burn.

"Blake was the name of the woman he cheated on Gretchen with."

"Oh my fucking God!" I screamed. "You're kidding me, right?" My breaths were burning my lungs as I gasped.

"I wish I were. But it could be a different Blake; there are plenty of women named Blake. Don't get too upset. You should really talk to him some more since this is bothering you so much."

I was close to blacking out from anger, and hate. I lowered my head into my hands and rubbed my temples. Tears burned my eyes. I held my eyes closed until I felt my mom's hand touch my shoulder.

"Nikki, you can't let yourself get upset like this. You have to think about the baby."

"I -- I think --" My stomach was churning, and I quickly darted down the hall to the bathroom to empty the contents. When I stood up, the rage and hurt were still there, along with some dizziness. I slowly walked back down to the kitchen.

"Are you okay? Maybe you should sit down."

I sat down. But I felt a tightness in my chest that extended down to my stomach. I was being kicked relentlessly by his baby, and my belly had tightened as if the muscles were being tugged tight. After a few seconds, the feeling left my body. The rage remained.

"Nikki."

"What?"

"What's wrong?"

"I don't know? I think I'm okay." Not even ten minutes after I was asked, that same tightness repeated its grip on my stomach.

The tightness in my stomach was coupled by a dull ache that wrapped around to my lower back. I sucked in a deep breath and grimaced. As quickly as the pain came, it was gone. I released my breath slowly as Mom watched me.

"I think maybe it was just a gas pain."

"Let"s hope that's all it was."

About ten minutes later, the whole grueling process began again. When I held my stomach in my hands, Mom screamed for Jim to come in the kitchen as she scrambled to get the phone and called for an ambulance.

The pain subsided, and I tried to reassure Jim and her that I was fine and to get them to cancel the ambulance. She agreed to it if twenty minutes passed and I didn't experience any further discomfort. Jim held Abby in his arms as she began to cry.

Like clockwork, the tightness and pain gripped me again not even ten minutes later. Abby wailed as if she were going through the pain. Just as the muscles relaxed, there was a knock on the front door. Jim went and answered it. The paramedics entered and began their inquiry. Within ten minutes they were able to witness another occurrence of what I tried to explain.

"It looks like you may be in labor, or hopefully only false labor. Either way, we should get you in to be observed and checked out. How far along are you?"

"Seven and a half months."

"It's a bit early for your baby to make his or her grand entrance. We need to get you to the hospital."

"I can't leave Abby."

"She'll be with us, and we'll be at the hospital shortly after you get there. You need to worry about the one you're carrying," Jim said. He was using his strength to keep Abby from leaning out of his arms to reach me. Mom grabbed her purse and keys.

Chapter 19

Mom came in the room and extended her arm toward me to hand me *my* cell-phone. I didn't even realize she had my phone.

"Hello?" I said hesitantly, while my eyes stayed fixed on Mom.

"Baby, are you okay? Your mom told me what happened. What's going on?"

A sudden flash of panic raced through me, causing my heartbeat to race. "What did she tell you?"

"She told me you were in the hospital. That you had gone into labor while visiting her." Jeff cleared his throat. "I'm so happy you were over at her house. I couldn't imagine what might have happened if you had been home alone, or at the store, or driving with Abby."

I was relieved to know Mom hadn't blabbed about our conversation. I didn't want to get into that right now. "I'm okay. The doctors said the baby is fine, too. I was given some medication to take from now until I'm two weeks from my delivery date. It's supposed to keep me from going into labor again."

After a few more minutes on the phone, I had convinced Jeff that we were fine and I'd be home the next day.

I only wished my mom hadn't told me about Blake and Jeff. It was eating at me to know what kind of relationship they had. Were they seriously involved or was it just a hook up?

The way she latched onto him at her house, I'd say she still had feelings for him. I wondered if that was why she had been at his house when he proposed. How many times had she been there? Did they have sex in the same bed Jeff and I shared now? Did he cuddle up to her, like he had done with me?

"Nikki," Mom called.

"Uh, sorry. Did you ask me something?"

"Jim and I are going to leave and take Abby home. I'll come back later if you like."

'No, that's okay. I'll be all right. You guys get some sleep. I'm sorry to be so much trouble. I'll see you tomorrow morning when I can get out of here."

Mom leaned down and kissed my forehead. "You aren't any trouble, dear, you can't control contractions. You get some sleep too. I'll be here early. I love you, sweetie."

"I love you too, Mom."

After they left, I flipped through the channels on TV. It seemed so weird not to watch Nickelodeon or Cartoon Network with Abby snuggled up against me.

Then I remembered, Sunday was Father's Day. Even though Jeff wasn't officially a father yet, he was a father-to-be. Sky would have Abby, of course, and I had to think of something for Jeff.

****

We began Father's Day with breakfast in bed. I begged him to have sex with me, but he insisted that we shouldn't. I had told Jeff the day before that the doctors had said to be careful; maybe I'd have been better off not saying anything. When we finally got out of the bed, I told him I needed him to get something out of my trunk. I walked down with him because I wanted to see his face.

When he lifted the trunk open, he had such a toothy grin on his face. He looked at me and laughed. "I have to work today?"

"I'll help you, but I couldn't carry it in the house by myself."

"I don't even know if I have tools for this."

"I bought those too. The salesman told me what we'd need and took me to find them." I put a hand on my hip, my big round belly jutting out in front of me. "No more excuses, mister. Get that crib out of there."

Jeff held me by my nape and pulled my mouth to his, his lips hovering over and grazing mine gently. "I love you, girl."

"I love you too."

Jeff

I didn't want anything for Father's Day. Knowing that Nikki was carrying my son was all I needed. I have to admit, she surprised me with the crib. I had planned on us shopping in a few weeks to get everything we'd need for the nursery.

And she had bought tools.

I was half tempted to call Connor or Hunter to come over and put the crib together for me, but I figured it might be more entertaining to let Nikki help me.

"Babe, grab that bag and let's go set this up."

I pulled the crib out and balanced it on my shoulder. It wasn't a heavy box, it was just awkwardly sized.

Nikki walked past me to open the door.

"Do you think we'll need anything else or do I have all the tools we'll need?"

"We'll find out in a few minutes, sweetheart."

"I have another question. Should we put the crib in our bedroom? At least for the first couple of months while I'm on leave?"

I turned slowly to look at her. She had no idea how beautiful she was. "That might not be a bad idea. But we have to move him out and into his own room before you go back to work." I heard the words leave my mouth, but I didn't even believe myself. Abby was in the room closest to ours. At best, if the baby moved, he'd be in the room with Abby.

"Come on, we have a job to do." I began walking down to our bedroom.

"You have work to do." I heard her mutter as she walked behind me. "It's your gift."

I pretended like I didn't hear her. I'm pretty sure she had intended for me to hear her comments. We walked into the bedroom, and I set the box down in the middle of the room. I had to get the box cutter, but first, I had something else to do. "You can set the bag on top of the box for now."

I sat on the edge of the bed. "Come over here, baby, I think I pulled a muscle."

"Oh, no." She walked over, and I pulled her so she was standing between my legs. "Can you massage it for me, please?"

"Sure." Her magical fingers felt so good on my shoulders and neck. I wrapped my arms around her and squeezed my legs closed around hers. Her scent was intoxicating. She had a faint smell of my favorite lotion, mingled with her own beautiful musk. I could see the slight perspiration glistening on her skin on her exposed chest and neck. A tingle shot through me from my stomach to my nuts.

"Does that feel good?"

"It feels great, baby." I had her locked in. She couldn't get away no matter what she tried. "So I heard you say this was all for me to do." It was at that time I could feel her tense and panic beginning to set in.

She laughed. "Yeah."

"That wasn't very nice of you, Mrs. Carrington."

"It wasn't meant to be mean, I was merely stating a fact."

"Oh, really?"

"Yeah, really." She started trying to wiggle free of my hold.

"Where are you trying to go, baby doll?" She was laughing pretty hard. She had such an infectious chuckle and occasional snort.

"You can let me go."

"Oh, I could, but I'm not going to. I'm going to make you pay for being a smartass."

I began tickling her. ""Stop!" she managed to squeak out between her giggles. "Jeff!" She tried prying my fingers from her ribs.

"Are you going to help me?"

She was wiggling and her arms were gripping my fingers while I tickled her relentlessly. "Answer me, baby. Are you going to help?"

She was laughing so hard she was gasping for breath. "I can go all night if you don't answer."

She screamed out forced words between her whoops and giggles. "I'm gonna pee."

"Then answer me." I leaned my head against her tummy. That made it impossible for her to have the leverage to work on my fingers.

"Yes!" she screamed wildly. "Yes, I'll help."

I held her tight to me. "That's all I wanted, a little cooperation." I laughed. Her hands slithered through my hair. I wrapped my arms around her, pulling her in to me, pressing her against me.

I slid my hands up her arms, grabbing her hair in each of my hands, and coaxed her down so our mouths met. She rested her butt on my leg, and I pulled her closer, tasting her lips with my tongue before consuming her. I wanted to eat her up.

She broke our kiss to plead. "Please, Jeff. I want you so bad."

"We aren't supposed to do anything that might affect you or the baby."

"I know my body. And I know what I want. Right now, I want you more than I want to breathe."

There was no way I could resist her after hearing her say that. I pulled her mouth back down on mine. My hands worked furiously to raise her shirt over her head, and then tossed it on the floor.

"You have to promise me, if this bothers you in any way, that you'll tell me."

"I promise." She pulled my mouth back to hers and wrapped her arms around my neck.

Chapter 20

"Baby doll, we need to talk. I don't know what's going on with you, but it has to be dealt with right now."

Jeff had been away the entire week, and had come in the house upset. I had a feeling he would. Each night we talked, I felt like I was on an emotional rollercoaster. I had worked so hard on Father's Day weekend not to let the thoughts of Blake ruin our time together, especially after being hospitalized. But every day this past week, I sat at my desk with my thoughts flooded with images of *her*, images of her wrapping Jeff in her tentacles, and, even worse, thoughts of them together in bed. That didn't make for too many pleasant conversations in the evenings.

When I'd get off the phone, I felt bad that I had been so snippy with him or had made some ridiculous excuse that I had to go.

"I really don't want to talk about it."

"That's just too fucking bad. I don't have the patience to keep going through this shit. When I call you, I can't wait to hear your voice. I want to talk to you. And when I come home, our house is supposed to be a place to relax, but I can't when I never know what I'm walking into with you." He crossed his arms and his lips thinned. "So out with it, right now."

I gulped. I didn't want to argue or fight. I was tired and would've loved nothing more than to take a nap. "Well, I --" I shifted my weight from one foot to the other. "I can't help but wonder what's between you and Blake."

He laughed. Not the reaction I had thought I'd get. "There's nothing between us, end of story."

I could feel my heartbeat in my throat. This wasn't going to be easy. "How long have you known her?"

"About four or five years."

"She's beautiful, Jeff. You mean you've never found her attractiveness too much to overlook?"

"Sweetheart, there is nothing between us."

Fuck, he's not going to tell me. I'm going to be forced to just ask and probably piss him off. I inhaled deeply and felt a sinking feeling washing over me. "Have you fucked her?"

"Are you fucking kidding me? What the fuck would make you ask me that bullshit question?"

My eyes prickled, and my breaths were forced in and out of my lungs. I felt unsteady. Unsure if I'd be able to continue to stand, I pulled out a chair and sat down. My tears were overflowing and spilling down my face. My chest was tight. I was at a loss; he was prepared to stand his lying ass ground and deny it until he died. He couldn't possibly think I was this dumb.

"Why were you two in that room, and why were her hands on you? You didn't even flinch." I couldn't bear asking the question burning in my head. I had too many other questions I wanted answers for and didn't want to ask that one just to have him storm off before I could get any answers.

"I don't know why she is so touchy-feely, but she's like that with everyone. We were talking about work. She had just found out she's being moved to another department."

My nose burned. "I didn't like her hugging on you when we got there, either." I dropped my eyes to the floor.

"Baby, I'm yours. I love you. Do you hear me? I don't know what is going on with you. Has this pregnancy got you that fucking insecure?" He walked over to me, placed a finger beneath my chin then lifted my face until our eyes met. "I fucking love you, woman. No one else."

My tears continued to stream, and I tried to control my sobs, but I couldn't.

"But," I croaked out. I didn't even recognize my own voice. "Fuck."

"Just say it, Nikki. I don't want to holler at you, but I'm not sure how much more of this I can tolerate." He backed away from me. "When this conversation ends today, this shit needs to be over."

My face heated and my pulse raced. Without any further deliberation, I blurted out the question that was at the crux of my angst. "Answer my question then. Have you fucked her? Ever?"

Jeff's silence and restlessness was the answer I didn't want. I felt sick. God knows I wanted him to say no, but I could tell that wasn't the answer.

"Oh my god, you did, didn't you?"

He dropped his hands to his sides, fidgeting with his pockets, and his gaze shifted away from me. "It's not what you think."

"How the hell do you know what I think? Oh my god! Oh my fucking God! Jesus, Jeff, why?"

"Nikki," He looked at me with a sadness in his eyes I had never seen before, "I swear, I never cheated on you."

My body heaved as the sobs shook me to my core. My ears felt congested, my vision was blurred by tears, and my entire body felt weak. If I hadn't been sitting, I might have collapsed. Jeff knelt in front of me.

"Baby, it was before us." He wrapped his arms around me, and pulled me into him, holding me tight. "I'm not going to get into it or discuss it, because it was years ago and only happened once. You have to know, from the time I told you I wanted to see you, there was only you."

My words were trapped behind the huge lump in my throat. Jeff held my face in his hands, tilted my head up, and gently kissed me. When I put my hands on him at his waist, his kiss deepened. He removed his hands from me, took mine, and pulled them to wrap around his core. He pressed against my belly as he moaned into my mouth.

He broke the kiss and peered into my eyes, "I'd never do anything to hurt you. Not on purpose anyway." A slight smile curled his lips, but his eyes still seemed sad.

"You aren't attracted to her anymore, not even a little?"

Jeff stood. "Fuck no, not even a little."

"But all the trips, had she tried to come on to you?"

"Yeah, she did. But I told her I wasn't interested. I told her I loved you. I told her before I had even told you."

"Why did she come to your party?"

"I have no fucking idea. She wasn't invited there, just like she wasn't invited to our wedding." He crossed his arms. "I think she's a kook. She's fucking nuts. I didn't want her trying to ruin shit for us."

I stood to get a glass of water. I'd kill to have a stiff drink right now. But I'd have to wait another month. Jeff's arm swooped me into him. "Know this, baby, there's only one woman for me. And that woman is you."

I was pulled into him tight, our tongues colliding, drinking him in. Letting him quench my thirst.

"Can we please be done with this topic?" Jeff asked as his lips lightly touched mine.

"Yeah." I had other questions, but I couldn't drag up his past, especially not things that happened before us. If I did, that meant my past could be exposed as well. I had no other choice but to take him at his word and trust him.

≈ Jeff ≈

If I had fucked Blake once or fucked her five hundred times, it didn't matter. The result would still be the same. Nikki still would have been pissed and wouldn't have liked the answer. So that little tidbit of information would stay my secret. It didn't matter how many times I had slept with her. I never fucked her while I was with Nikki; that was a fact, and that was what mattered.

The truth was, my cock had found solace in Blake after breaking up with Gretchen. What I hadn't realized was that I was trading in one nut job for another.

Gretchen never seemed to enjoy sex. Being with her was like being with a dead fish. She just laid there. She didn't like giving head, and she didn't seem to enjoy getting fucked. She wanted to talk. *Talk, talk, talk, talk, talk.* I wanted her to shut the fuck up. It got to a point where I found no pleasure at all in even being around her, so I cut her loose. Unfortunately, she didn't accept the break-up. I couldn't have been clearer, but she pretended like we were destined for a life together. When she walked in on me pounding Blake, she finally got the hint.

Blake was the complete opposite of Gretchen. She loved sex and would do anything and everything to please me. I remember when she was hired as an administrative assistant, how she'd bat her long eyelashes at me behind those fucking school-teacher glasses. Every day, she found some way to interact with me on behalf of our mutual boss. My cock would perk up at the sound of her voice, but I fought the urge to act upon that impulse.

Connor and several others had warned me not to shit where I ate, and to leave her alone. It was easier to walk away while I was still wasting time with Gretchen, but the moment we broke up, I couldn't resist her any longer. I was going to take her out to dinner, but we never made it out of my car. She gave me a blow job right after I parked at the restaurant. I didn't finish in her mouth, like I had wanted to. Instead I held out until I took her back to my place and fucked her brains out right in the foyer.

I had forgotten to lock the front door. I didn't think I needed to.

Enter Gretchen, the psycho. She tried to cause a bit of a scene, but I didn't stop fucking Blake, so Gretchen eventually stormed out.

Blake liked to talk, but she was easy to shut up with my dick jammed down her throat. I loved the way her sexy, luscious, made-to-fuck body responded to me buried in her orifices. It didn't matter if I was taking her mouth, her pussy, or her ass. She writhed and bucked beneath me like an insatiable beast. Then she lost her mind and told me she thought she loved me. That made me realize I had spent far too much time with her. I had to cut her loose. I didn't love her; hell, I really didn't even like her. I just liked to use her.

It was about a month after I had cut all ties with her that she was promoted into the open position and would be part of my team. I'd have to travel with and train her. She saw it as a second opportunity. I saw it as a fucking nightmare.

When I started dating Nikki, the green-eyed monster reared her ugly head and tried every trick in the book. I shunned every advance she attempted. Eventually, she got engaged to Jason. I never even knew they had gone out. Perhaps she thought I'd be jealous and that would get me back, but I had fallen in love with Nikki by then. I always knew Jason was weak and pathetic, but for him to fall into her web proved it. She was never getting her claws in me again.

Now this brazen bitch practically threw herself at me in her own house, in her bedroom, with her husband, whom she admitted she didn't love, not far away. In front of my wife. She had no regard for her own marriage or mine.

What was confusing me right now was who the fuck had told Nikki I had slept with that she-devil? Whoever it was, they obviously didn't know everything where Blake was concerned, which was a good thing. I could only hope nothing else from my past would be dragged to the surface.

My baby doll was like a piece of fine China. She was fragile. She needed to be shielded. The slightest little bump could knock her off balance and break her. I couldn't bear the thought of that.

Chapter 21

Before Jeff left for his next stint out of town, he had insisted I give serious thought to hiring someone to come in to help watch Abby, and help me around the house. He told me I could have someone live there if I felt comfortable with them. He thought that would be better than just someone to come in daily. I really didn't think I needed someone long-term. At most, I thought just long enough to help out while I was on leave.

I placed an advertisement on that Monday morning, and the next day, I received a call from a woman named Estelle. She sounded older, but it's hard to tell over the phone. She was going to meet Abby and me at McDonald's. I didn't want her to come to the house until I had a chance to see her and feel her out. I also wanted her to see how energetic Abby was. If I got a weird vibe from her, I'd keep looking.

My meeting with Estelle was, um, interesting – not! As I had suspected, she was an older woman. She told me she was sixty-nine years old. I admired her willingness to work, to watch a toddler, but she was visibly agitated watching Abby run back and forth between the play area and me. She kept looking like she wanted to say something each time Abby ran up to the table. She also sat in her seat clutching her purse like it was her lifeline.

I thanked her and told her I would be in touch by the end of the week. I already knew there was no way she would be the person to watch Abby, but didn't want to tell her that while we were in public. I'd give her a call on Friday and let her know my decision.

As soon as Abby and I got in the car, my phone rang. It was another person answering my ad. She asked if we could meet that same night. She was out running errands and would meet anywhere I chose. I was put on the spot; I really wanted to go home. Instead, I told her I would meet her at the mall, since that was one of the stops she rattled off that she had to make a trip to.

Abby and I parked and walked in and made our way to the food court. I described myself to Jessica, and she told me what she was wearing. I felt like a creeper when a woman walked by dressed similarly to what was described, but it wasn't her. The woman looked at me like I was violating her with a glance. *Bitch*.

"I want to go home, Mommy."

"I know, baby, we'll be leaving soon."

"I want to go now."

"Don't do that, please. I don't want to hear you whining."

I was saved when a stranger dressed exactly as described walked up to me. "Nikki?"

"Hi. Yes, I'm Nikki. And you must be Jessica?" I stood to greet her.

"Hi, yes, I'm Jessica. And this must be Abby."

"That's her; she's not shy, though." Abby had her face buried in my arm, peeking around slightly at Jessica.

"Hi, Abby." Jessica smiled. She was young.

Abby gave Jessica a small wave.

"How old are you?"

Abby held up four fingers.

"Do you talk yet?"

"Yeah!" Abby screamed and began laughing.

"Thanks for meeting with me on such short notice, Nikki."

We sat in the mall and talked for nearly an hour. I explained what I was looking for and the limited time we would need her. She was fine with all of that. I asked her if she was opposed to living in our home during the time she'd be helping with the kids, and she wasn't since her lease was coming to an end. I told her we might consider extending the time for the position, but that hadn't been decided yet. I'm not sure why I said that.

Jessica was twenty-one years old. She was in school for nursing, but felt it really wasn't the desired career path after getting half way through the curriculum. Her parents were livid and not thrilled about her coming home. She loved children, and Abby really was drawn to her when we met.

I told her I'd need to have a background check done and would let her know hopefully by the end of the week. I really liked her.

We kept wine and hard liquor in the house, so I needed to make sure the person I hired was of legal drinking age. Also, I heard too many stories of husbands cheating with nannies. Not that Jeff was around much, but when he was, I didn't want him looking at anyone else lustfully except me. Maybe that was another reason I liked Jessica. She wasn't super pretty and she didn't have a slim body, but she was such a nice person. I don't want him to be tempted by anyone. One woman like Blake to deal with was more than enough for me.

I was surprised I had only received two other phone calls about the advertisement. The interviews over the phone eliminated both of them, and we never met in person. I knew in my heart, Jessica was the right person.

On Friday morning, I received a call from one of the attorneys Jeff had suggested with the results of Jessica's background check. Her background was squeaky clean, so I asked her to come over on Saturday to the house. She could see where we lived and meet Jeff.

When she arrived on Saturday, Abby was glued to the television, watching Sponge Bob cartoons. Jeff and I were sitting in the kitchen. We both had agreed we would not make a decision while she was in the house. We sat and talked to her for about twenty minutes before Jeff decided he'd had enough and announced he was going to take a drive to Connor's place. He grabbed a handful of my hair, tilted my head back, and kissed me. I loved when he pulled my hair. I never wanted any other man to pull my hair, but Jeff could without any objection from me. He released my mouth, grabbed his keys and disappeared through the front door.

Jessica and I talked for a few more minutes. Before she left, I assured her I would let her know our decision by Monday.

Jeff and I agreed to hire her. He didn't say much about her, but he asked a lot of questions to make sure I was really ready to pull the trigger. He told me we should draw up a contract to make sure the estimated date to end her time with us was clearly spelled out and she knew to find another job and another place to live by then.

He wanted me to seriously consider keeping Jessica until the baby was a year old, but I wasn't ready to make that long of a commitment. In two or three months, I could come to hate having her around, or she could change her mind about babysitting for us. I wanted to make sure we all still got along before extending the length of the job.

After Jeff left for his trip, I gave Estelle a call and let her know we had selected another candidate. Immediately, I called Jessica. She was ecstatic. I'm pretty sure she was jumping up and down wherever she was. She sure as hell squealed in my ear.

We agreed to her moving in on the weekend after I found out she was living with a friend.

Chapter 22

The more I thought about having someone come in the house to watch Abby, the more I thought it was a complete waste of money. And pretty damned ridiculous. I was more than capable of taking care of my own child.

I sat at my desk and shrugged my shoulders and shook my head as I pulled up the next account. I had two more weeks until my due date. My goal was to get everything done so when Robert stepped in to take over, he would start with a clean slate.

With everything that had been going on, I was surprised I hadn't made any mistakes that would have had Jack running to my desk or calling me into his office. I was happy, but surprised.

"You've been really elusive lately."

I looked up from my monitor into Georgia's prying eyes. "Hey. I don't mean to be. You know, it's just getting really hectic."

"I'll take your word for it. I've never had the first-hand experience of being pregnant, married, and all that other jazz."

"Yeah, the scare of going into labor early had Jeff in a tailspin. We just hired a short-term nanny to come in and help out."

"That's not a bad idea. When you come home from having the baby, she can help get Abby off to school and pick her up. Plus, you can get some sleep because you're going to need it."

"You're right. I guess I didn't think about all of that. She will be more beneficial after I have the baby."

"Are we going to lunch today? We need to catch up."

"Absolutely; let's go."

"I'll make sure to get Candace, and we can head out at noon."

"Sounds good. Stop by when you guys are ready."

"Sure will."

It was noon before I knew it. Candace and Georgia walked up and were standing by my desk, waiting for me to lock up my computer and get my purse.

"Hey Momma. Are you ready to go?" Candace asked.

"I am; let's go."

We walked down the hall to the elevator, then made our way out of the building and across the street. We were on a mission to get some pizza. My food choices were mainly pizza and McDonald's. No wonder I had gained nearly fifty pounds already. With two more weeks, I would easily top fifty. That was a depressing thought. There wasn't anything I could do at this point to lessen the weight gain, though. I just had to prepare to work really hard to get the weight off after the baby was born.

"Have you and Jeff given any idea to names?" Candace asked.

"I have, but I haven't talked to Jeff yet. I don't want to say anything until we talk and he agrees."

"Just tell us what names you've been thinking about," Georgia prodded.

"I've given some thought to Jeffrey Jr., Sam, Aiden, Collin, Bryson, Chase, and Alexander."

"Oh, those are all nice names. It's going to be hard to pick from them," Candace said.

"Thanks. I'll make sure you guys know as soon as we make a final decision."

"Cool. And you're working all the way up until you have the baby?" Candace asked.

"Yep. I want to have all of my maternity leave after I have the baby, not waste days before sitting around the house watching daytime television."

"I can't say I blame you. I'd do it the same way if it were me. It would suck to take off based on your due date, then find out you don't have the baby for two more weeks."

"Jeez, Georgia, don't jinx me like that. I shuddered at the thought of being pregnant for another four weeks, ugh. I'm so ready for him to evacuate the premises." We all laughed.

"Were you on-time or late with Abby?" Georgia asked.

"I was a day beyond the due date with her. I can only hope to be that close this time around."

"We better get back. We can't let you get in trouble before going out." I laughed at Georgia. I doubted very much that I'd get in trouble for being a couple minutes late getting back from lunch, but I didn't want to get back late anyway. I had a stack of work to get done.

****

The weekend was upon us before we knew it. I had met with Jessica on Thursday after work so we could review the contract and get her signature. Jessica called early Saturday morning to let me know she was on her way. Her call came earlier than I had expected, but I didn't mind getting an early start to the day. Abby woke up and ran down the stairs. Miss Nosy. She was excited to see Jessica and couldn't wait to take her up to show her the room she would stay in. She was going to be on the other side of Abby, away from our bedroom.

It was great Jessica didn't have any large items or furniture to move. We had a bedroom set in the room she would stay in. She came in with a few suitcases and a couple duffle bags full of clothes.

Once she got all of her things up to her room, I took her on a full tour of the house. Abby tagged along behind us.

"This house is so amazing." We made our way back into the kitchen where I started a pot of coffee.

"Thanks. Do you have any questions for me at all?"

"No, nothing that I can think of."

"Jeff will be home later this morning. He's done traveling until about a month after I have the baby." I was very happy that he wouldn't be traveling for a while. The transfer for that she-devil Blake hadn't been finalized. I hated that she was still on the road with Jeff. No matter what he wanted to think, I knew she still had a thing for him. The thought of them being away for three or four days really bugged the hell out of me. I could see her subtly flirting and throwing herself at him. I wished I had never met her.

"Okay. Maybe you can tell me some things you'd like me to do. Or things you expect from me. I don't want to disappoint you guys. I want to be as helpful as I can."

"I think a lot of your assistance is going to be needed when I go to the hospital and when I come back home. Sky, my ex-husband and Abby's father, takes her every other weekend. If I'm in the hospital over a weekend, he's going to take her during that time. I'm going to need you to make sure she gets to day care and back during the week, though. Monday, I'll make sure your name is on the list of approved people to pick her up and drop her off."

"Will you need help with cooking? I love to cook."

"Jeff will need you to cook; he is very limited in the kitchen."

"How about cleaning? I can do the housecleaning starting now." She looked around. "But there isn't a whole lot to do; the place is pretty clean."

"There's a cleaning service that comes in every other week. They do a pretty thorough job, but if you can help make sure things are kept picked up, that would be great. Abby knows how to pick up her own toys. She doesn't like it, but she knows how, and she should be made to do it instead of you doing it for her."

"Okay, that's no problem. Oh, grocery shopping. Do you want me to do that?"

"Sure, that would be great."

The more I sat and talked to Jessica about what she should do, the more ridiculous I felt having her here. I know Jeff was looking out for me when he said to find someone, but the amount of work I was able to delegate to her didn't seem significant enough to justify hiring her. At least I wasn't paying her an exorbitant amount of money. Her agreeing to live in for the few months reduced the weekly pay.

We sat and chatted for another hour or so. I was so tired, even the caffeine couldn't keep my eyes open.

"If you want to go lie back down, I can watch Abby."

"You don't mind?"

"That's what you're paying me for. I may as well earn my keep, right?"

"Thanks. I have been so tired with this pregnancy. I wasn't like this with Abby."

"It happens. My sister was like that with her youngest. She couldn't get enough sleep. Don't worry, I'll get her fed and we'll be fine."

"Well, I'm going to take you up on your offer. When Jeff comes home --." I stood from my chair.

"I'll let him know you're lying down."

"Abby, be good for Miss Jessica, okay?"

"Yes, Mommy, I'll be good."

"I'll see you guys later." I walked up the steps to my room. I closed the door and pulled off my clothes, then slid in under the sheet.

I felt the bed sink on Jeff's side, then I felt the warmth of his body pressed against my back. His arm wrapped around my body, and his hand rubbed my belly. He moved my hair, and I felt his warm breath on my neck, sending chills down my spine. I loved when he crept in the bed with me and held me tight to him.

I rolled over and felt the sheet and pillow were still warm on Jeff's side of the bed, but he was gone. I sat up, slid my feet over to the floor and stood to get dressed and go downstairs.

"Where are you going?" Jeff's voice startled me.

"I thought you had left the room."

"No, baby doll, I just had to piss." He stalked over toward me and stopped right in front of me. He cupped my head in his hands and leaned in to kiss me. I melted into him. I loved having him at home. And to think -- I'd be wrapped in his arms every night for the next six weeks.

Chapter 23

A couple of weeks after Jessica moved in with us, my water broke, and I was taken to the hospital. I was quickly admitted and moved into a room. My contractions hadn't even started yet, but they got the IV going, and the anesthesiologist was ready to begin Pitocin to induce me, if needed. Poor Jeff sat helplessly quiet and watched the nurses come in and out of the room to gather additional information.

The monitors were hooked up to me to collect statistics on everything. I didn't realize I was considered a high-risk pregnancy until then. Evidently, because I had gone into labor early, that afforded me the new label. My obstetrician was also concerned that the baby was near ten pounds, if not a little more.

Since I was not making good progress with labor on my own after an hour being in my room, they went ahead and induced me.

It took about an hour after they gave me the medicine before the alarm rang on the blood pressure monitor to notify the nurses. There was a dangerous spike in my numbers that I was told not only threatened my life if they didn't get it lowered, but it was a concern for the baby. When I asked what their comments meant, I was told it could mean the baby was in distress or that something else may be going on. The nurses tried to move me onto my side to help drop my numbers back to normal, or at least closer to normal. Within thirty minutes, the numbers decreased, but not enough to satisfy the doctor.

Jeff sat by my side, rubbing my hand. "Baby, do you feel stressed? Are you okay?"

"Well, yeah, duh, I am now," I snapped at him. I didn't mean to take it out on him. I knew he was just concerned. "They tell me something may be going on with the baby; that's pretty fucking stressful. Before they said that, I felt fine. I had a headache, but other than that, I was okay."

"The doctor will be in to check on you in a bit. We need to try to get your blood pressure down some more, if possible," the nurse said as she wrote on my chart.

I was having a hard time staying up on my right side, so the nurse propped pillows behind my back before leaving us alone.

"I'm so thirsty."

"Sorry, babe, you can't have any water, only these ice chips."

The contractions were picking up in intensity and frequency. They were about eight minutes apart when the doctor came back in my room.

"Well, Nikki, let's check your blood pressure again." He watched the monitor as the machine displayed the numbers. "Here's my concern," he began. "You're blood pressure is abnormally high. Throughout your pregnancy, your blood pressure stayed pretty normal."

"So what does that mean?" Jeff asked.

"We're going to give Nikki some medication to try to lower the numbers. If they don't drop in another half hour to an hour, we'll talk about next steps. So before we get too excited, let's see what we can do about getting them down."

"Thanks." I was getting nervous. I didn't like the way this was going. The last thing I wanted was for something to happen to my baby. Our baby.

The nurse came back in with two small paper cups; one of them had two tablets, and the other had about a swallow of water.

I choked down the pills and laid back down. Jeff held my hand, and I whispered to him, "Now I'm feeling really stressed. I don't like this at all."

"Just try to stay calm, baby. Everything will be okay." Jeff stood beside me, leaned over, and kissed my forehead. I could see the tension in his facial expression. He didn't believe the words that said to me. He was every bit as stressed as I was.

It took the doctor about an hour to come back in to check on me. When he looked at the blood pressure readings, he cleared his throat, turned to look at me, and then quickly returned his gaze to the printout.

"We need to discuss options, now," he said without turning to face us.

He pulled over a chair near my bed and sat. "Your blood pressure isn't cooperating like I had hoped. Let's discuss a C-section."

A tear trickled down my temple. *Fuck, I didn't want to get cut.*

"Are there any other options?" Jeff asked.

"We've tried the anti-anxiety meds, but they didn't work. I'm afraid the longer we wait, the more compromised the baby could be. I wish there was another alternative, but unfortunately, there isn't. I really don't want to give more medications because everything we give Nikki does affect the baby."

Jeff stroked my hand. I swallowed hard. I was choked up on this. Anything they had to do to make sure the baby was fine, I'd do it. I'd never be able to live with myself if anything happened to him.

Jeff looked at me, and I knew we were both thinking the same thing. Neither of us liked that option, but since there weren't any other good choices, I had to do what I had to do.

"Fine, let's do it." I managed to squeeze the words out past the lump in my throat.

Jeff stood and kissed my dry, chapped lips. "I love you, baby."

"I love you, too."

A nurse came in and began prepping me for my surgery. Once they had me ready, they wheeled me down to an operating room. Jeff was at my side the entire time.

Alexander Jeffrey Carrington did not come into this world easily. It was a struggle the entire four hours of labor. It got so bad, I was begging them to hurry up and do the cesarean section to get him out of me. I had no idea how Jeff's fingers weren't broken from my excessive squeezing while I waited for the epidural to kick in. Yet, when the doctor confirmed it was a boy, we both shed tears of joy, and the pain I had endured was so worth it.

Jeff had immediately expressed his fear for Alexander's health. The doctor assured him they were going to run tests and monitor him.

Mom was in the operating room with us as backup. I needed her there. I really didn't know how much support I was going to get from Jeff, honestly. He had surprised me, though; he was there and eager to do whatever I needed.

We all had laughed when the doctor asked if he wanted to cut the cord. His reply was a drawn out, emphatic, no.

The nurses weighed the baby and announced he was ten pounds and seven ounces. He also measured twenty-four inches long. *He was huge.*

The doctor explained to us that the umbilical cord had been wrapped around Alexander's neck. Natural childbirth could have been very dangerous for him. Tears streamed down Jeff's face, which, in turn, caused my tears to flow even harder.

The nurse handed our wonderful little boy to Jeff. My mom took pictures of Jeff holding Alexander. It was the most precious sight ever.

"Baby. He's perfect." Jeff said. He couldn't stop staring at Alexander.

I got to hold him for a few short minutes, then, they whisked our son away, and the emptiness left me feeling hollow.

Sky and Hope had called Mom to check on me and told her they we're going to bring Abby up the next day so she could meet her baby brother. I wanted to see her, but I was exhausted. I wanted nothing more than to go to sleep.

I muttered to Jeff, "I love you."

Jeff stroked my hair, then kissed my forehead and temple as my eyes closed.

Jeff

Nikki's water broke at home. Luckily, she was standing in the kitchen on the tile floor. The doctor was on his way to the hospital while the nurses checked, poked, and prodded at her. And I breathed with her like she was taught during Lamaze classes. I got really lightheaded and thought I was going to pass the fuck out. I guess I should have paid more attention.

I sat in a chair beside the bed, quiet as a mouse, holding and stroking Nikki's hand. Her agonizing moans in between erratic breaths during each painful contraction made me feel helpless. I would have given anything to take her pain onto myself, sparing her. My only comfort was knowing it would eventually be over.

Nikki's mom and Jim arrived. Rebekka coddled and rubbed Nikki's hair, smoothing it down and asked how she was doing and how far apart the contractions were. Just before Nikki replied, the doctor and nurse entered the room, asking everyone to please step out briefly so they could check her. I stayed. Fuck that. She's my wife, and this was my baby.

When everyone returned, the doctor announced to them that Nikki was going to be given some meds for her blood pressure. He seemed pretty optimistic the meds would help, until he returned an hour later and the optimism had vanished. Jim let Rebekka know he was going to step out of the room and return to the waiting area. Rebekka showed concern for me; she said I looked exhausted.

"Neither of us slept well last night," I told her. "The baby was kicking like crazy. It was when Nikki got up to get a drink of water that she screamed for me because her water broke."

"You'll both get plenty of time to sleep in about eighteen years." Nikki's mom chuckled.

"Nikki, it won't be much longer, hang in there." Her mom stroked her hair and face again.

"I can hardly take this shit anymore. And I couldn't even get anything for the pain because the contractions are getting too close." Tears streamed down Nikki's face. I gently wiped them away with my hands.

The doctor and nurse returned once again to check Nikki's progress. It wasn't good. Her blood pressure was still too high, and they wanted to do a C-section. I wanted them to do whatever was best for both of my babies. I couldn't take the thought of anything happening to either one of them.

Once Nikki gave the go-ahead, the nurse pulled the curtain and began prepping her. The nurse handed Rebekka and I our garments to change into.

They finished her up pretty quickly, then we headed down to the operating room. Nikki begged that both her mom and I be allowed to come in with her, which the nurse agreed to. I was going to be by Nikki's side no matter what; hospital security couldn't have gotten me away from her. She needed me. And I sure as fuck needed her. The nurse handed both of us our garments to change into as she prepared to get Nikki down the hall.

Shortly after we were led into the room for the delivery, we heard her scream, "Just get this baby out of me already!" We both looked at each other and smiled. The anesthesiologist was at the ready, shushing her, telling her to hold still and not to scream so she could rid her of her pain.

After they gave Nikki the shot in her spine, it didn't take long.

"Congratulations, it's a boy!" the doctor announced.

Nikki and I just stared at each other, and tears streamed down both of our faces. We knew we were having a son, but something about that announcement from the doctor shook me to the core.

I had never been happier. I was a dad. We were parents; we had a son. I confirmed and reconfirmed that he was healthy, with ten fingers and ten toes. The tears continued to stream down our faces, and Nikki's mom was equally ecstatic.

"A grandson," she sighed out.

The nurse announced his weight and height. Alexander was a big boy. He weighed in at ten pounds seven ounces, and he was twenty-four inches tall, two feet already. *That was my boy.*

The doctor explained to us that Alexander had the cord around his neck and told us what could have happened if he had been delivered naturally. My heart stopped. I felt gutted. I could have lost my son. The tears fell.

I would have felt ashamed any other time to be seen crying so much, but this was a special situation. One I had never thought in a million years I'd be experiencing.

When I held my son in my arms, and looked at his face, my heart was full of more love than I've ever known. The one thing I said I didn't want was the one thing I now wanted more than anything else in the world.

After talking with Nikki for a few minutes more, Nikki's mom suggested I go get some sleep, then return in a couple hours. She was going to leave as well, but would make sure to come back up the next day. That would also give my beautiful wife, the love of my life, a chance to get some rest.

I couldn't leave her all alone here, though. I planned to go to sleep in her room, while she slept, and then, when her mom came back, I'd leave.

Chapter 24

The doctor came into the recovery room the morning after the baby was born with a frown on his face. His eyebrows were furrowed, and he walked over to the edge of my bed, next to Jeff.

"Well, I have some good news and some concerns to share with you both." I took in a deep breath. The doctor reached his hand out and laid it on Jeff's shoulder. "We don't have any sign of jaundice in Alexander. And for the most part, everything looks good."

The doctor dropped his hands and slid them in his jacket pocket, rattling his keys or change, or whatever was in there.

"I'm not sure how much we need to worry about this right now, but we've detected a mild arrhythmia. I don't want this to be too alarming to you, though; sometimes they will go away as children age. But we definitely want to keep a close eye on him and monitor him monthly, after you're back home. We'll keep watching him while he's here, hoping for signs of improvement, and we'll talk to you before you leave."

I looked up at Jeff and saw that his face had lost all hint of color; he was as white as a ghost. I felt completely helpless.

"When can we see him?" I asked. I'm sure Jeff wanted to know the same.

"We will finish the couple remaining tests and get him right down to you."

"Thank you."

"Try not to worry; we'll make sure little, well, I mean not so little, Alexander, is well taken care of." The doctor chuckled at his light-hearted pun. "We have a pediatric cardiologist who will come in to see him. Once they run their tests, we should have a better idea what we are facing and how we should proceed."

Jeff stood still like a statue.

Jeff

My heart stopped when the doctor said Alexander had an arrhythmia. *What in the fucking fuck?* How is that shit fair to my baby? An innocent baby?

I couldn't take it if anything happened to him. I loved him so much my own heart hurt. As much as the doctor wanted to keep us calm, my mind was racing a mile a minute, and not with good thoughts.

Nikki was doing a whole lot better than I was. Her strength was amazing. Me, I was reduced to a puddle of mush. I felt like if I moved at all, I'd collapse. I felt like I needed to get out of there, but I couldn't leave her. I didn't dare leave her, not all alone, not now.

"Baby, I think when your mom comes up, I'm going to leave for a bit."

"That's fine. I'll be here when you come back. Are you okay?"

"I'm not sure right now. I can't believe he has a problem."

"Well, baby, try not to get too upset yet. I want to hear what the cardiologist has to say."

"Yeah." I heard her talking, but I didn't have her ability to remain calm. I wanted to punch the fuck out of something.

Nikki looked at her phone when it beeped. "You know, if you want to take off, you can; my mom is on her way."

"I think I will. I'll be back in a couple hours." I bent and kissed her forehead. "I love you, baby."

"I love you, too."

****

I drove to see my mother. I needed to talk to her. My mind was stuck on the doctor's words: *we've detected an arrhythmia*. I slammed my hand on the steering wheel. *Fuck!* What if it turned out to not be mild like they thought? What if it was life-threatening? What if he needed heart surgery, or worse, nothing could be done for him? The tears were building up in my eyes, and I shook my head as I continued to drive to Mom's house.

I pulled into her driveway and slammed the car into park, then jumped out and walked up to her door. I knocked briskly, and the door was opened right away.

"Hey, Jeff, what brings you by? Where's Nikki?"

"Hi Karen, is Mom here?"

"She's in the kitchen."

"Come on, I'll tell you both the good news at the same time." Karen was like a sister to me. I didn't have any siblings, but we got really close when she started taking care of Mom.

She followed me into the kitchen. I walked over and hugged Mom and kissed her cheek. "Hi, Mom."

"Hi, darling, how are you doing? No Nikki today?"

"Well, that's actually the good news. Nikki is in the hospital. She had the baby. I was going to call you, but I really wanted to come deliver the good news in person. Congratulations, you're a grandmother."

Mom's lip quivered even as she smiled. "Congratulations, but shouldn't you be with her?"

"Her mom is there. I'll go back up after I shower and eat."

"Tell me about the baby. What name did you guys pick? How much did he weigh? How long was he? And what time was he born?" By the time she finished the onslaught of questions, she was teary-eyed.

"Alexander Jeffrey was ten pounds seven ounces and twenty-four inches long. A whole two feet, can you believe it, mom? He's huge and he was born just after five am. That was why I didn't call."

"You can call me anytime of the day, you know that." She waved her hand in the air dismissing my excuse. "Alexander, I like that name. I can't wait to see him."

"They'll be in the hospital for a few more days. Nikki had to have a C-section. Her blood pressure shot up and –" I choked on my words.

I could feel my emotions balling up in my throat. I walked over to the cupboard to retrieve a glass. I needed something to drink. I'd have loved nothing more than a stiff shot of whiskey, but Mom didn't keep alcohol in the house. Just as well, especially today.

"Is everything okay, Jeffrey?"

I turned to get the pitcher of juice out of the refrigerator and half-filled my glass.

"Can I get you something to eat?" Karen asked.

"Sure, thanks, Karen." I sat down at the table with Mom.

"Tell me what's going on, dear. You have worry all over your face and that's scaring me."

I set my elbows on the table and buried my face in my hands. "Oh, Mom," I muttered into my hands.

I dragged my hands down my face, wiping the tears from my eyes. "I -- I --"

She reached over and held my hand in hers. "Darling, is everything okay with Nikki and the baby?"

"Nikki's fine. It's Alexander." I dropped my head. "I'm so scared right now, I don't know what to do or what to think."

"What happened to him?"

"The doctor said they detected an arrhythmia." I slammed my fist on the table. "Jesus, Mom, I'm so scared that this will end up being bad." The tears were streaming down my face. My heart was crumbling. "I couldn't take it if anything happened to him." I sniffed and wiped the tears from my face just as a plate was set in front of me.

I wasn't hungry. How could I eat?

"Sweetheart, are there any specialists looking at him?"

"They have a pediatric cardiologist coming in to look at him. The doctor said not to get too upset, but he's my son. How am I supposed to not get upset?"

"Jeffrey, you need to try to calm down and stay positive. Just wait until you hear what they say. Everything is going to be fine. You'll see."

Mom patted my hand. "Eat your food, dear; you need your strength. You have to be strong for Nikki."

Chapter 25

By the time Jeff returned to the hospital, Gary and his wife were sitting in my room. He and his family had planned to come home in a couple weeks, but figured this was the perfect time. He wanted to stop by to see me and meet their new nephew, my son, Alexander. They came directly to the hospital instead of going to our mother's house. It was just as well, since Mom was still at the hospital with me. Mom sat in the waiting area with their twins, but Bianca came in with them to see me.

After a couple of hours, Mom handed Gary the keys to the house so they could let themselves in. Jim had gone out to run errands and might not have gotten back home. She also wasn't ready to leave.

It seemed like only minutes after Gary's family left before Sky, Hope, and Abby were in the room. I helped Abby sit on the bed near me, and I was letting her hold Alexander, with my help, of course. It was the cutest thing, seeing her hold him. Jeff and Sky both reached in their pockets and pulled out their phones. It was like being in a photo shoot, with all the camera phones being directed at us and photos being snapped.

"Take him, Mommy."

"Okay, baby." I slid Alexander out of Abby's arms and into my hands. I winced as a pain shot through my stomach. Jeff walked over and took him from me.

"Do you like your new baby brother?" Jeff asked. He stood holding him in one arm like he was a human football.

"Yep, he's a nice baby."

"Do you remember his name?"

"Alexander."

"So how are things going with you two?" I said as I looked at Sky and Hope. They both looked at each other, and I was pretty sure I saw the eye-twinkle and sparks fly between them.

"Things are going good with us."

We all talked for a few more minutes before the nurse came in and asked to take Alexander down for his screening with the cardiologist. Jeff handed him over to the nurse, who laid him in his bassinet and wheeled him out of the room.

"What's going on?" Sky asked.

"They found that Alexander has an arrhythmia. They're doing some extra tests with a cardiologist to make sure it's not something we need to be too concerned about."

"Damn, I'm sorry to hear that. Hopefully it's not anything serious," Sky said.

"Aw, Nikki, Jeff, I'm so sorry to hear," Hope chimed in. She was so sugary sweet, yet sincere. No wonder Sky liked her. And she was so gorgeous.

"If this helps put your mind at ease, Gary had an irregular heart beat when he was a baby, too." Mom sat up and scooted to the edge of her chair. "By the time he was three, it was gone. He never had any problems, but he was checked during his regular visits to make sure everything was okay." Mom's comments helped more than she knew. I saw Jeff the tension in Jeff's shoulders ease after hearing what she had to say.

"We know you need to get some rest, Nikki. Congratulations again to you and Jeff." Sky shook Jeff's hand and gave me a quick hug. Hope gave us both a hug, too, then Abby came over and gave me a hug.

"Come on, little Abby girl, time to go home." Sky held his hand out for Abby.

"No, I want to stay with Mommy." She was gripping my arm tight.

"Baby, you can't stay with me. I have to stay in the hospital a couple more days. But you can come see me again tomorrow."

"Okay." Her lip quivered and pulled down into a frown.

I reminded Sky that Jessica was home if he needed to drop Abby off.

Right after they left, the nurse brought Alexander back down to the room. She told us the doctor would be down to discuss any findings momentarily. My mom jumped up and was quick to scoop him up out of the bassinet before Jeff could get to him. She went and sat back down in her seat, cradling her new grandson in her arms.

"You know, he looks a lot like you already, Jeff. All he's missing is the beard and mustache."

Hearing my mom make the comment reminded me that, somehow, I had to figure out how to get a DNA test done. I was ninety-nine percent sure Alexander was Jeff's son, but I needed to be one hundred percent sure. I wanted no doubt in my mind, ever.

Jeff was going to be home for the next thirty days, so I'd have to wait until he went back to work. That would give me more than enough time to figure out a plan.

"Did you hear me, dear?" Mom asked.

"I'm sorry, I was daydreaming, and I didn't. What did you ask me?"

"Do you have godparents picked out for Alexander?"

"Nothing that we've talked about. I don't even had godparents for Abby. Maybe Jackie could be both of the kids' godmother."

"That's one. Who else would you choose? Normally, the godparents are a couple."

I shrugged my shoulders. "I don't know."

"Well, you have some time to figure that out, but just something to think about, in case anything happened to you both, God forbid."

The last thing on my mind was finding godparents for my kids.

I looked over at the clock. Time was flying by; it was almost six o'clock. I heard a light knock on the door just before Jackie and Mandy came in the room.

"Hey, Nik, how are you feeling?" Jackie walked over and gave me a hug.

"Hey, Nikki, you look very beautiful," Mandy said and gave me a quick little wave.

"I was beginning to wonder about you two. I'm so happy you both came up."

"Hey, Jeff, how are you holding up?" Jackie asked as Mandy gave him a quick hug. "How's it feel to be a dad?"

"I'm doing fine, tired, but what can I do? It feels great being a father. I had it easy, though. All I had to do was let Nikki break a couple fingers." He smiled. *God, he was gorgeous.*

"Nikki, baby, I'm going to run. I'll be back up tomorrow. I need to get home. I don't want to leave Gary and his family there for long alone in case they need something."

"Thanks for coming up, Mom. Tell Jim I said hi."

"I will, sweetie." She gave me a hug and kiss, then walked over to Jeff and gave him a hug, too.

She tapped him on his chest. "Take good care of my little girl."

"I always will. She's worth more than gold to me."

Mom smiled at him, rubbed his arm, and then picked up her purse. She said goodbye to Jackie and Mandy before she left.

As soon as mom cleared the doorway, Hunter and Connor joined all of us in the room. They both did the whole high-five, handshake thing with Jeff, then each gave me a hug. Jackie was holding the baby when they walked in. Hunter's eyes were drawn to her as soon as he stood up straight.

"You look like a natural holding the baby," he said to her.

"One day, one day." Her eyes were fixed on him.

We all talked and laughed for an hour before our four visitors decided it was time to go. They all walked out together, leaving Jeff, Alexander, and me, in the room. Alexander was getting cranky, which I knew meant he was hungry. Jeff handed him to me. I was breastfeeding him. I knew it was the best thing for him, at least until I was ready to return to work.

"You're so beautiful, baby. I could just sit and stare at you all day."

I could feel the heat rise in my neck and face. I looked like hell. I was still overweight, and my hair was a mess. I felt like I had to have had bags under my eyes. On top of that, I didn't have any make-up on. "Thank you."

Jeff came over and sat on the bed next to me, stroking my leg over the cover. "I meant what I said to your mother. You mean the world to me, Nikki. You have no idea how happy I am." His eyes were glassy, filled with tears, tears that never spilled down his cheeks.

"I am, too." I was not so fortunate as to have my tears hover in my eyes. They made a jagged path down my cheeks and dripped into Alexander's hair.

Chapter 26

Visitors continued to flood in and out of my room like it had a revolving door all the way up until the time the doctors released me a couple days later. I'm sure the nurses were glad to see me leave.

I was able to get around pretty good, considering every muscle in my stomach felt like it had been cut and ripped from my body.

We got some pretty reassuring news from the cardiologist before I was released. They confirmed the arrhythmia was mild. I asked if it was possible it would be outgrown, and they said they had seen that before, but they couldn't say that was going to be the case. They didn't want to give us false hope. They were very guarded in their responses to us. They planned to run some more tests when he was six months old to see if he was getting better, stayed the same, or if the irregularity had gotten worse.

Before we both left the hospital, they taught us CPR so if there were any issues once we got home, we would be able to tend to him while waiting for a medical team. The thought of administering CPR to my own son terrified me. They told us both it was good to know in general because you never know what a little kid can get into. That didn't help me much.

It felt so good being back at home, though. The more I looked at Alexander, the more I saw Jeff. He had a lot of dark hair, more than I would have expected for a baby, and definitely more than Abby had when she was born. His eyes matched Jeff's. They weren't open much, but when they were, my heart was pierced by his intense bluish-greys.

Holding him was surreal. I had never expected to have another baby, especially not after the talk with Jeff about how much he didn't want kids. Then, when Jeff reacted so badly, I was terrified I'd lose him and I'd be left to raise two kids on my own.

Not only did we have the crib in our room, but we had a new chair. It was a really nice, wide chaise lounge. Jeff told me he had it delivered while I was in the hospital. When I was woke up in the middle of the night and early in the mornings to feed Alexander, Jeff would sit on the chaise with me, holding us both. Sometimes I could hear his breathing even out and he'd occasionally snore, but it was so relaxing, so peaceful knowing he was there with us. It just felt so perfect. But his remaining time at home with us was slowly dwindling. He only had a month off for paternity leave.

Jeff was right, too. Having Jessica here to help was fantastic. She helped get Abby up and fed in the mornings, then took her to school. And she was prompt with picking her up.

After the first two weeks of being at home, I went back to cooking dinner. I had to do something to make myself feel normal and to get back into the swing of things here at home.

****

The night before Jeff was to return to work left me in a deep funk for so many reasons. I didn't want him to leave. I didn't want him to travel anymore. I didn't want him around Blake. He told me that was who he had to go out of town with and that this was supposed to be the last time, but that didn't settle the uneasy feeling in the pit of my stomach. I sat in the chaise as I watched my husband pack to leave for a three-day trip with the she-devil herself.

Alexander was incredibly cranky, too. He wouldn't stop crying, and that wasn't helping me at all. He was fed and changed, but all the patting him on the back and bouncing him on my leg did nothing to soothe him. Maybe Alexander knew we should all be sitting on the chair, not just the two of us. Maybe he didn't want his daddy to leave him, either.

I stood and paced around the room with him, which seemed to help. But it did nothing to calm me. I had hoped so desperately that Jeff would be able to work from home and no longer have to travel weekly. I wanted that in the worst way so he could be home with me, but it didn't happen. He was assured it was only a matter of time and in a couple months that should be his new reality. He was going to begin training his replacement so he could stay in the corporate office and, at some point in the near future, work from home a couple days a week.

My heart was breaking more and more with each passing minute.

"I'll be back in a few days. I'm not leaving forever."

It seemed like it to me. I fought back the tears. "I know."

❧ Jeff ❧

I could see the sadness on her face, in her eyes, but there was nothing I could do or say to comfort her. I had to leave. I had to get back to work. We both knew up front that I was only going to be off for a month. Hell, if I had my way, I wouldn't be leaving. I'd love nothing more than to stay here with her and Alexander.

But I knew she'd be fine in time, and she'd adjust to me being gone again. I wasn't looking forward to leaving and being back on the road, but there was solace in knowing it wasn't forever. It was just a matter of time and I'd be home every night, sleeping in my own bed, spending time with my family. Like a normal family does. But until then, I had to keep doing what was necessary to make sure the bills were paid and my family was provided for.

"I'll be back in a few days. I'm not leaving forever." I hated seeing her like that. But I also knew she wasn't being left alone. She had Jessica here with her.

"I know." I could tell by her voice that she was near tears, and thank fucking God she didn't start crying. I needed her to keep her shit together so I didn't have to try to deal with that on top of everything else going on in my mind.

Alexander was going to the doctor while I was gone, and the thought of those results terrified me. I had hoped with all my might that he was better and they wouldn't hear the irregular heartbeat, but in my own heart, I knew that probably wasn't going to be the case.

They were going to check to make sure there were no blockages in his arteries. That would eliminate a lot of concern, but it still wouldn't give us the answers we needed. We still didn't know if he'd need to be put on medication or not. I was hoping not.

Chapter 27

I fought like hell to prevent tears from being shed as I said good-bye to Jeff. Watching him walk out the door was harder than I had ever expected it to be.

Who would have guessed him being off from work for a month would have had such a powerful impact. But sleeping in his arms, sitting on the chaise while feeding Alexander, just going through all of the day-to-day activities with him had changed me. And it confirmed that's what I wanted.

As soon as Jeff's car began backing down the driveway, the tears fell. I felt empty. And lonely. The next three days would feel like an eternity. I hated the thought of not talking to him in person, not seeing him.

But more than anything else, I hated that he was going to be with her. She had already tried to come on to him when they traveled. The brazen bitch even tried to come on to him right in her own house. With her husband and me both there. She had no concern for anyone but herself, and she seemed to be pretty hell-bent on getting what she wanted, which was my husband back in her web.

I stood with my head leaning on the doorway, staring at the empty driveway. He was gone. I released a deep sigh. I had to pull myself together. Alexander had his visit with the doctor later. Mom was going to drive me to the appointment.

I felt helpless. I couldn't drive myself anywhere yet. I had a live-in babysitter for Abby to help me get her back and forth to day care. To justify Jessica's presence, she was getting Abby up in the mornings and cooking her breakfast. She was also making sure Abby was bathed at night because leaning over the tub with these stitches was impossible.

I couldn't even work out. I had only lost nineteen pounds when I had Alexander, so I still had thirty-five pounds to lose. Because of the C-section, I couldn't do anything to help me lose weight except starve myself. *But that won't happen. I'm not big on starving; that's why I'm fat right now. And Blake is perfect. And she's with my husband.* I dropped my eyes to the floor, shook my head, and closed the door.

My chest felt hollow. It felt like my heart had been ripped from my body. I wanted to go back to bed and never get up. I just wanted to pull the sheet over my head and fall into a deep coma-type sleep. If I didn't have children, I could do that.

And if I didn't have Alexander, I'd be going to work, and my life would be normal. And I wouldn't have to go to the pediatrician. And I'd be driving Abby to school. And I wouldn't be fat. And I --

I felt the hand on my arm, then turned my head to face her. "Nikki, do you want some breakfast with Abby?"

"I'm going to just have coffee. Thanks." I had lost my appetite.

I followed Jessica into the kitchen and poured a cup. I sat at the breakfast bar next to Abby, who was eating home-made waffles that smelled absolutely divine. I slumped down, and rested my head in my hand. My arm was bent at the elbow, and propped against the table.

"What's wrong, Mommy?" The corners of Abby's mouth were turned down, and she was rubbing my hand that rested on my coffee mug handle.

"Nothing, baby, I'm just tired."

"You should go take a nap."

"I will. Eat all your food so you can be smart in school."

"I am. I'm real smart, Mommy." She removed her little hand from mine and grabbed her fork. All in one motion, she shoveled a huge bite of waffles into her mouth. I couldn't help but smile. She looked like a chipmunk.

"I know, baby. I know." I raised my mug to my lips and sipped my hot beverage.

By the time my mom had arrived at the house, I had taken a shower, washed my hair and pulled it back into the worst-looking ponytail ever, and fed Alexander. I was looking at myself in the mirror when the doorbell rang. I had on one of Jeff's T-shirts and a pair of my sweatpants that had become a staple of my nine-months-pregnant wardrobe after coming home from work. I wanted to break the mirror so I'd never have to see myself again. *How in the hell was Jeff still with me? Look at me! Why would anyone who looked like him want to be with someone who looked like me?*

I had only gained thirty pounds with Abby, and the weight had dropped off so fast. By the time I went back to work, I was able to fit into all of my pre-pregnancy clothes. Judging by the way I looked now in my reflection, when it was time for me to go back to work, I'd need them to relax the dress code for me so I could wear those funky gray sweats.

I wrapped the blanket around Alexander and carefully walked down the stairs into the kitchen.

"There you are. How are you doing today, sweetie?" Mom's smile was wide as she held her arms out to take the baby from me.

"I'm fine. Tired. I'd love to just sleep the rest of the day."

"Well, Alexander, that wouldn't be fair to you, now would it, my little cutie pie?" Mom stood there and had Alexander smiling and wiggling in her arms as she talked to him. He really responded to her.

"Shall we get going? We need to go make sure this precious baby is going to be fine."

"Yeah, let's go. I sure hope that's what they say."

****

By the time we returned home, Jessica had already brought Abby home. She ran to my mom as soon as we walked in the house. Fortunately for my mom, I was holding Alexander, who was fast asleep. *Lucky him.* Mom talked to Abby as I went and laid him down upstairs and turned on the monitor. I retrieved my phone out of my pocket and sent a text to Jeff. He was probably in a meeting, and I didn't want to disturb him. I would have called if I had some super great news, but I didn't. There wasn't much of a change. They did say the irregular beat wasn't as easily detectable, but it was still there. I had an appointment to go back in another month.

The next appointment, I'd be able to drive myself. It would be two months; there was no way I was going to be confined to the house for more than two months. I had scheduled the appointment for later that afternoon, too.

I had a plan. I was going to pick up Abby, then take her with me to the doctor's visit. While there, I'd talk them into swabbing both her and Alexander to compare their DNA. Mine will be there for both, but the paternal DNA should be different. I had done enough research on the Internet to know I didn't need Sky or Jeff. Luckily for me, I had Abby.

Chapter 28

The weeks dragged on. The repetition in my daily life was driving me out of my mind. I felt like I had no purpose. I had started working out, against my doctor's orders, but only doing very light things. A lot of walking and some low-impact aerobics. I could see a difference, but I still had quite a few extra pounds that were clinging to my body in all the wrong places.

I had called Jackie a few times, but the best I could get out of her was a text conversation and the promise she would come see me one of these weekends. *What the fuck!*

Mandy came by a couple times. She let me know she and Creighton were back together. I was happy for her. And Georgia and Candace had come by several times to check up on me and filled me in on the office gossip.

And while all that was just fine and dandy, this was the big day. Alexander was going to his follow-up visit and I was going to convince the doctor to do this test and keep it a secret. No one could ever know.

Ever.

"Are you sure you don't want me to come with you?" Jessica was standing in the kitchen, looking bored as hell, as usual.

"No, I won't be gone long. I need to get out of the house and do this."

"Well, if you need anything while you're out, give me a call."

"Thank you, I will."

I picked up my keys, the diaper bag, and Alexander, then headed out the door.

After picking up Abby, we went to the doctor's office. They went through the routine of checking Alexander like the last time.

"Have you noticed any abnormal behavior?" the doctor asked me.

"No, he's happy and seems to be fine."

"Yes, his heartbeat seems a little closer to what we would consider normal. It's very possible that by six months, this will all be a distant memory." The doctor picked up the chart and began writing his notes. "We will still need to check him monthly until we are certain everything is fine."

"I understand; that makes sense."

"Did you have any other questions for me today?"

"I had one." Abby began coughing as I spoke. *Perfect timing.* "I think Abby may be coming down with something. Do you think you could swab her mouth, then compare it to Alexander for me?"

"Are you asking me to do a --" I cut him off before he said the test out loud. Abby was in the habit of repeating things, and that was one thing I never wanted mentioned in the house.

"Yes, doctor, I am. That's exactly what I'm asking you to do." I did everything except steeple my fingers as I pleaded. "Please, I desperately need you to do this for me."

"And I'm assuming this must be completely confidential?"

"Absolutely."

"Fine. I normally wouldn't do this. I would typically send you to a lab, but I'll do this for you this one time."

"Thank you. I appreciate this more than you can imagine."

"You can call my nurse on Friday after three pm to get the results. I'll mark the chart to make sure no one calls you and that they only speak with you about this test result."

"Thank you so much."

The doctor left, and I gathered up my babies. Abby tried to carry the diaper bag for me, but it was weighing her down on one side. It was so cute to see her struggle with it. We went out, and I made a follow-up appointment for Alexander. I wanted to get him in to be seen before I went back to work. It was easier that way. I wouldn't have to take time off work right away.

I sent Jeff a text as soon as we got in the car. I didn't expect him to reply. I just wanted to give him the update. We could talk later that night.

Chapter 29

The week went by extra slow, but the day had arrived for me to call and get the results of the DNA test. My hands were sweaty, and my heart was racing as I dialed the numbers. I shouldn't have been so nervous. One look at that little boy's face was proof whose son he was. This call was just confirmation. *But there was still that slight chance Sky was the father, and that's what scared the hell out of me.* How would I react if that were the result? Would I scream and run to a couch, burying my head in the cushions, like on Maury? Would I pass out? One thing was for sure, I'd be moving out, and my life would be wrecked.

"Doctor's office."

"Good afternoon, this is Nikki Carrington. I was calling about a test result for my son, Alexander." I confirmed his birthdate and everything else she asked for.

"One second, and I'll go pull his chart." I was put on hold and left there for-fucking-ever. Obviously, they didn't realize the longer I sat on hold, the closer I was to having a heart attack from anxiety. I inhaled deeply, then slowly released my breath.

"Mrs. Carrington," the nurse said, "we have the result."

"I'm ready." I was sitting on the bed, staring in toward Alexander's crib.

"The tests between your daughter and son do not match." I collapsed on the bed, the phone was glued to my ear. I released the breath I hadn't realized I was holding.

A weight had been lifted from my shoulders. "Thank you."

"Was there anything else you needed today?"

"No, that was it."

"Have a nice day."

I hung up, then pounded my fist into the bed. I would never, ever do anything that careless again. Never.

I walked over and picked up my sleeping baby into my arms and hugged him tight. Relief flowed through me. I was freed.

****

The days seemed to fly by. It hadn't taken me very long before I got used to Jeff leaving every week, again. Jessica living with us helped keep me from feeling lonely. It was different with Abby and Alexander, too. They kept me so busy sometimes I didn't have time to think of anything else except them and what they needed.

Each week had become as repetitive as the last, but I found ways to improve my mood. I had taken it upon myself to do more for myself. I was driving myself around and even drove Abby to day care and picked her up a couple days a week.

My depression faded after I began working out. I had been working out consistently, slowly increasing the intensity. I was returning to work the next week and had only ten pounds left to lose.

Alexander was almost three months old and had his third checkup since being home. He was getting so big, and his arrhythmia was improving each time we went, or at least that's what I had been told. I was relieved that they said they didn't think there was a need to medicate him.

I asked Jessica to stay with us an extra couple of weeks after I returned to work, until the day care was able to start watching Alexander. I hated having him there so young, but Abby went when she was very young, and she was fine. They took very good care of the kids they watched, and I had known them for years.

I had my final doctor appointment to get my checkup before being released to go back to work. I had been looking forward to Jeff coming home, too. I was looking forward to getting back to our normal sex life. I loved giving blow jobs, but enough was enough now. I was excited to get back to normal. I needed that desperately. We didn't have anything special planned for the coming weekend, all I knew was I was hell-bent on spending at least two hours of quality alone time with my man. I was so happy Jessica was still living with us.

I was up to date on all the office gossip, thanks to Candace and Georgia. There wasn't a lot going on, but Jack had started dating someone and was trying to keep it secret. Little did he know, everyone knew.

****

Being at work the first few days had been nothing more than showing pictures of Alexander and Abby, catching up with everyone, and basically, being retrained at my own job by Robert. He had made so many updates to the processes that I felt like I was in a completely new position.

We were going out for happy hour after work. We had decided going on Thursday would be better than Friday. Plus, Georgia had a date Friday night. That alone was surprise enough, then she told me she was finally going out with Connor. I was shocked. I preferred Thursday as well. Jeff was going to be home Saturday morning for sure, but said he'd try to get there Friday night. If he came home Friday, I wanted to be home to see him.

Keeping Jessica the extra couple of weeks was such a smart decision. If she hadn't stayed on, I wouldn't be able to go out with all my work friends. I didn't plan to stay out late, but it was nice to engage in adult camaraderie again.

"So what can I get you all tonight?"

"A glass of Chardonnay, please." This was my first drink of alcohol since the bachelorette party drinking debacle. But I was going to enjoy this glass of wine; I was looking forward to tasting it. My mouth began watering. I knew I'd only have two glasses, I couldn't overdrink. It had been a long time and I wanted to ease myself back into drinking. I could always have another glass when I got home, if I wanted one. Alexander's sucking had become so intense, leaving my nipples raw and bleeding, that I had stopped breastfeeding a couple of weeks before I went back to work.

Everyone else ordered, and it didn't take long before our drinks were brought out to us. We had the complimentary chips and salsa to munch on as we talked and drank. After about an hour, Jason, Jack's brother, and *her* husband, came in and joined us at our table.

Within a half an hour everyone except Jack, Jason, and I had left.

Chapter 30

Jason being in the bar that night felt strange. The only time I had been around him before that night was at the cookout at their home, with her, his wife the she-devil.

Jason had been getting pretty hammered. I was sitting inside the booth near the wall, beside Jack. When I excused myself to go to the bathroom, Jason jumped up from his seat and was face-to-face with me where I stood.

"You aren't leaving, are you?"

"Not yet, but soon. I'll be back."

"Good, we have more to talk about." *What the hell was this guy's deal?* I had thought I was done talking to bar drunks when I met Jeff. Something about his tone resonated in my head and had me on edge. Why would *we* have more to talk about?

I returned, and Jack stood to let me slide in. I didn't plan to stay much longer. I needed to get home. It was a little after seven o'clock, and the thought of being here listening to Jason's drunken diatribe didn't excite me in the least.

"How's that wonderful husband of yours, and the baby?" Seriously? I clutched at my purse; I was ready to leave.

"My husband is fine. And Alexander is perfect. How could he not be?" *Fucking asshole.* "How is your wife?" I felt like we had begun a sparring match. I didn't want this. I didn't want to talk about my family to him, and I damn sure didn't give a rat's ass about his bitch wife, Blake.

"I don't know. I'll ask her when she gets home. She's out of town right now. She's been gone all week."

My stomach sank. *Did he just say what I think he said?*

"Oh, I'm sorry. By the look on your face, I'm guessing Jeff didn't tell you they were out of town together, again." He waved his hand flippantly in the air. "On *business*."

I sat frozen to my seat, my head slowly shaking back and forth. This couldn't be. He had told me he was going to be with Sandy before he left. Why would he lie to me? I had talked to him the past nights, and he never mentioned it then, either. I picked up my glass and coaxed the last couple of drops of wine from it into my mouth.

"Can I get you another drink? You're probably going to need it." How could he sit there with such a smug look on his face? What a fucking dick. He waved for the waitress, then asked her to bring us all another round. Until he ordered for Jack, I had completely forgotten he was sitting right next to me.

"There's a lot you don't know, sweetheart. I can tell you, if you like. I can tell you everything. And I plan to. It's about time someone tells you the truth." His wink at me was pure evil.

"Where to begin, hmm, at the beginning, I guess, is as good a place as any." Jason downed his shot of Tequila and took a draw of his beer as a chaser. My eyes were fixed on him. As much as I loathed his presence and didn't want to hear anything he said, I had to know.

Jason started by telling me Jeff's name had been tossed around as a possibility for a promotion to the position he was currently in. He had been considered for that same job a couple years earlier, but a couple of the senior managers thought he was still a bit too much of a wild card. They preferred someone who was more settled.

"We had all heard the reference to being settled and knew it meant to be either married or engaged." Jason took a drink of his beer. "He had just broken up with Gretchen. At about that time, he was pretty hot and heavy with Blake. Everyone knew it."

I swallowed hard. I didn't want to hear anything else about him and Blake.

"Then, all of a sudden, out of nowhere, you appear in the picture. I later found out Connor had spotted you for his boy and had given you his business card."

"How do you know that?"

"Connor can't keep his mouth shut. So, anyway, Jeff wasn't going to go out with you, but Connor kept nagging him."

"Why? Why would Connor care so much?"

"Connor was hoping that Jeff would do what he had to do, get the promotion, then he'd get him transferred over to his team."

"What do you mean, *do what he had to do*?"

"I told you, he had to be settled in the eyes of senior management."

Jack interrupted the two-way conversation. "Jason, that's enough."

"I told her I was going to tell her the truth. What I'm saying is one hundred percent the God's honest truth." Jack shrugged his shoulders and shook his head. He had a look on his face that said he tasted something rotten.

"Didn't you think it was even the least little bit strange how fast he was moving? How fast he moved you in with him?" Jason took a long draw of his beer. "Jesus. Come on. You can't be that stupid."

Jack interrupted his brother again. "That's enough, Jason. Just stop."

"Fuck it, she has a right to know the truth. Don't you want to know, Nikki?"

"Um, I don't think –"

"Sure you do, you know deep down you do. Hell, you probably already suspected some of the shit I'm going to tell you."

"Jason, for God's sake, just shut the fuck up."

Jason stood from his seat. He pointed a finger in Jack's face as he held his bottle of beer in the other hand. "Don't ever tell me to shut the fuck up again. I swear to Christ, if we weren't in this bar, I'd punch you right in your pussy-assed mouth."

Jack slumped back in his seat, letting his brother prove that not only was he older, but also the more dominant of the two. Jason sat back down.

"So as I was saying, sweetheart," he said. "Your husband, Mr. Fucking Perfect, isn't as perfect as he wants you to think."

Jason was drunk. Not falling down stupid drunk, but he'd had more than eight bottles of beer and had been doing shots. I really didn't want to listen to him talk shit about Jeff. "Look, Jason, seriously I don't --"

"You're going to listen to me. You want to hear what I have to say." He took another draw of his beer, then motioned for the waitress to come over. "Don't you want to know how that perfect husband of yours got that promotion?"

My heart sank. My thoughts immediately went to wondering who he'd had sex with. Then I recollected his manager was a man.

"Don't hurt yourself thinking, sweetheart; trust me, I'm going to tell you."

The waitress showed up, and Jason ordered another beer. Jack and I both passed.

"I asked you earlier, don't you wonder why he moved you in so fast?"

"No, I never gave it any thought beyond what we talked about. I'm not sure what this has to do with anything."

"I'm going to connect the puzzle pieces for you, Barbie. Answer this question, if you can. Did you think it was strange that the day he proposed, he just so happened to have a party that included his manager?"

"Jason, you really are fucked up. I'm leaving because I'm ashamed my brother is such a douchebag." Jack stood up and fished his keys out of his pocket.

"Sit back down, Jack; don't you dare try to leave." Jason's lips thinned, and his eyes were slits as he glared across the table. Jack lowered himself back into his seat.

"It was after that proposal that Wonder Boy got his promotion, right?"

"I think so."

"No, Nikki, you know so. You are the reason he got that job. You and the ready-made family you provided him. He was passed over the last time they were looking to promote someone."

My stomach sank. My chest ached.

The waitress returned and set Jason's new beer on the table and collected his empty bottle, then left.

"My darling wife, who wasn't my wife at the time, went by her lover's house because she couldn't believe he would stoop so low. But he did. He stooped to an all-time low, even for him."

I was stunned.

"You were the 'stable and secure' he needed to get the job he desperately wanted. He wanted it so bad, he married you."

I couldn't wrap my head around what I had just heard. My mouth went completely dry, and I gulped at the air to refill my lungs.

"But ..." I didn't know what I even wanted to say or ask. I was flabbergasted by what Jason was saying.

"I know, sweetheart, but he said he loves you. Do you really think he loves you, loves you? Or does he love you because he needed you and, well, now he just has to find the right way to get rid of you?" He took a couple swallows of his beer. "I have to hand it to you, you threw him a game-changing curve ball with the baby."

I ran my fingers into my hair. This couldn't be true. There was no way Jason was telling me the truth. But why would he lie?

He ran his hand over my hand that was lying limply on the table. I grabbed his hand and shoved it off me.

"Bottom line, darling, if Wonder Boy had his way, he'd still be pounding Blake. But she's my wife now." I raised my eyes and looked at him. I could feel the tears burning in my eyes. Jason gave me a smug smile and a wink.

"But with all these trips they take together, I wouldn't be surprised if they weren't still sleeping together. And why not? It's not like we'd ever find out, right? Not unless one of them was stupid enough to tell." He was a douchebag like Jack said.

"Remember the picnic at our house?"

I nodded my head. I couldn't forget about that day, no matter how hard I tried.

"Well, your husband cornered my wife. In *our* bedroom of all places. And that fuckwad actually had the nerve to disrespect my house and my marriage by making suggestive comments to Blake."

The tears tumbled down my cheeks. My worst fear was true; he did still desire her.

"I need to go," I said softly. My heart felt like it had exploded into tiny bits in my chest. The blood was rushing through my veins, causing my body and head to thump with each heartbeat. I picked up my purse. My vision was clouded by the heartache, and I could barely hear Jack call my name over the thuds in my ears.

I looked at Jack, but was unable to force words out.

"Are you going to be okay?" His hand touched my arm. I could hear that asshole Jason still blathering in the background. I slid across the seat until I found myself standing. I nodded my head before turning and walking toward the door.

I could hear Jack and Jason hollering obscenities, but I had to leave.

I was digging in my purse to find my keys. My sight was so muddled by the tears that were falling uncontrollably.

"Nikki." I looked up and saw Jason walking toward me. I swiped the tears away as best I could.

"Hey, look, Nikki, sorry I dumped all of that on you. I thought you had a right to know the truth, and clearly, he wasn't going to be the one who would tell you."

I just stood and stared at him. The words I wanted to say wouldn't come out. *Fuck off, Jason!*

He laughed. "Maybe we should ditch those two and let them have each other. They deserve each other anyway. You and I, we're runners up. We are nothing better than second place to them. As nice-looking as you are, you can't top her on your best day. You have to admit, she is fucking absolutely beautiful."

Was he seriously continuing to rub this in my face?

"Maybe you and I could give it a go, see what happens. It can't be any worse than what we have now."

I resumed the search for my keys. I had to get away from him. Once I had the keys in my hand, I unlocked the car. Before I could open the door to get in, Jason wrapped his arms around me and forced me into a kiss. I held my lips tight together. I pushed and hit him to get him to let me go. With one of my hits, I jabbed the key into him.

"Fucking bitch." He shoved me back against the car and walked away.

I opened the door, dropped into the seat, shut it, and dropped my head onto the steering wheel, and cried.

What did my life mean?

Chapter 31

I don't even know how I got home. My vision was blurred by the tears that never stopped. Everything had been perfect yesterday. It was perfect before I went to *un*happy hour. I couldn't believe that filthy bastard had the nerve to suggest we 'give it a go' and then kissed me. After everything he had said. Then that?

I unlocked the door and crept into the house, hoping not to alert Jessica that I was home. I wanted to go give Abby a kiss, then go hold Alexander -- the game-changer as Jason referred to him.

I retreated to the master suite to shower and wash my hair, but instead, saw Jessica sitting in the chaise giving Alexander a bottle.

"Hi," I gasped out. My voice was shaky and cracked.

"Nikki, what's wrong? You look like you've been crying."

My legs felt like they were going to give out. I sat on the chaise beside her while running my fingers through Alexander's hair. I sniffled and fought back tears.

I shook my head and just told her someone from the bar had said some really hurtful, shitty things to me. She pried gently, but I avoided giving her any details. I didn't know what I was going to do, but the last thing I had wanted was to retell the horribleness I had just heard. I told her I just wanted to shower, then I'd take Alexander from her.

I stood like a zombie in the shower as the warm water washed over me. My mind was replaying the events from the time I met Jeff. The first meeting in the restaurant had left me with a feeling that he wasn't interested in me. And that card, the business card given to me by Connor – he was in on this the whole time. Why didn't I just leave him alone? Why didn't I throw his card in the trash like I had done so many before him? Why did I chase after him? I broke every one of my own rules. And I had ignored every single red-flag.

I remembered us dating, if you want to call it that. The memories flooded back into my brain -- the day I told him about Abby, his reaction to kids, when he asked me to move in, how he proposed at that party with only his work friends in attendance. Connor the con-man, pretending to like me, and flattering me. The voice in my head had one word for me – *fool*! My hands trembled. *Oh.my.god! Jason was right.*

I wanted to believe everything was perfect. Our wedding day was perfect, wasn't it? Maybe I couldn't see the forest for the trees.

I was seriously questioning Jeff's feelings. I thought back to my pregnancy and how upset Jeff had been when he found out. When I caught Jeff in that room talking to Blake in secret, and him wanting to put me out on the side of the road because I questioned him. The devastation when I found out from my mom that Blake was the person he had cheated on Gretchen with. And all the trips he took with Blake. And now this? What was I thinking? I couldn't believe I had thrown myself at him. That I let him treat me the way he did. When had I become so desperate?

And then tonight, without warning, the rug was just ripped from beneath my feet, dumping me on my ass into a puddle of reality shit. I couldn't believe I allowed myself to love him so much. My heart hurt.

I could hear my phone ringing. I knew who it was, and he was the last person I wanted to talk to.

When I exited the bathroom, Jessica had the baby in his crib, fast asleep, but was sitting on the chaise with her legs crossed at the ankle, staring at me. I looked in her direction, but didn't really see her clearly.

"Did something else happen, Nikki? You don't seem to be the type of person who would let a few inconsiderate words upset you."

"I don't want to talk about it. I can't."

"When you need to, or want to, let me know. I'm here for you." She stood from the chaise. "Alexander is asleep, and so is Abby."

"Thank you, for everything."

She left my room and pulled the door shut behind her. I flopped on my bed and sobbed.

My phone rang again. I lifted my head, and for a moment, actually thought about answering his call. No matter how much I wanted to hear him tell me this was all a lie, I knew he couldn't do that. I let his call go to voicemail, like the earlier call had done.

I had to talk to someone, and the only person I wanted to talk to was Jackie. I called her and left a vague, yet urgent, voicemail. If she called me back at three in the morning, I'd answer.

Since I had my phone, I listened to the voicemails Jeff had left. Baby this and baby that. "Call me. I want to hear your voice. I love you." *Fuck you, Jeff. Fuck you and all your lies.*

****

I woke up to the alarm clock blaring, Alexander crying, and Abby trying to beat down my bedroom door. When it rains, it pours. I turned off the alarm, scooped up Alexander onto my hip, and turned the handle to let Abby in.

"Are you going to come eat breakfast with me, Mommy?"

"I'll be right down, baby."

I looked at my phone. Two more voicemails from him, but nothing from Jackie. Seeing his name in my list of recent callers made me take in a deep breath. I was fighting every urge to call him. But I wasn't ready to talk to him.

I bounded down the stairs into the kitchen with Alexander's plump little body on my hip, grasping my arm tight. If our relationship had meant nothing else, at least I had a beautiful son. He was mine forever.

I set him in his high-chair and took my seat next to Abby. A plate of waffles had been set there for me, while she and Jessica had already begun eating theirs.

"Feeling any better today?" Jessica asked.

"No, not really." I shoveled a fork-full of waffles into my mouth. They were so good.

"Are you sick, Mommy?"

"No, baby, just a little headache."

I turned to face Jessica. "Sky or Hope will be picking Abby up today," I said in a matter-of-fact way after I swallowed my bite of food.

"I remembered."

I broke off a small piece and fed it to Alexander. He loved the taste and began banging on the tray and making little grunting noises for more. I jammed another small piece in his mouth just as my phone rang. I glanced down and saw it was Jackie. Just the person I needed to talk to.

We talked briefly and in code. She had the day off and was going to come over. I wasn't going to work. I couldn't. I couldn't take the thought of Jack trying to explain away his brother's actions and words.

When Jackie arrived, Jessica was gone taking Abby to day care, and she was going to go to the grocery store to pick up some things for dinner. I spilled it all to Jackie. Every single bit of information Jason had shared. By the time I finished, my body was shaking, and I was sobbing hard into my hands. I felt the same as I had the night before, when Jason told me. Worse. I was reliving it all over again.

I asked Jackie, "Could it really all have been a lie? How could someone be so cruel? Why? All for a job promotion?" I sobbed for several more minutes into Jackie's shoulder as she rubbed my back. "What kind of heartless person does that?" I screeched out through my tight throat.

Jackie tried to comfort me. "You're going to have to talk to him eventually. Why don't you talk to him tonight?"

"I can't."

I felt like I couldn't breathe. My chest was so tight. Tighter than it had ever felt before. I was gasping for my next breath, and if I didn't have Abby and Alexander, I wouldn't have cared if my next breath came or not.

"I'm going to get you a drink of water, then we can keep talking. Okay?"

I nodded my head. My mouth was dry, and my throat hurt from all the tears and gulping. When Jackie left me, I laid my head down.

Jackie walked back in with two glasses of water at the same time my phone rang. I refused to answer Jeff's call, again.

"I don't want to be here when he gets home. I can't be, Jackie." I was rocking back and forth and wringing my hands.

"You aren't thinking straight. What are you going to do? Where are you going to go?"

"I don't know, but I won't be here. Sky and Hope have Abby for the weekend."

"What are you thinking? You have a devious look in your eyes."

"I have to get away from here. I need to go somewhere far away so I can think."

Jessica walked in and saw us sitting on the couch. I looked over at her and blurted out my question. "Hey, Jessica, you ever been to Vegas?"

"You have got to be kidding, Nik. No way," Jackie said.

"What's going on?" Jessica asked.

"Why not? Fuck it. I'll be gone all weekend and come back in the middle of next week."

"What about your job? Did you forget about that?" Jackie was being the voice of reason. She didn't realize, I was broken and beyond reasonable.

"They survived without me for three months, another few days won't hurt." I took a drink of my water. "Besides, it will give me some time to figure out what to do."

"What's going on?" Jessica asked again.

"Go pack up; we're going to Vegas tonight, and we'll be back on Wednesday. I'll get my laptop and find us some tickets."

"Nikki, seriously? I don't think this is a good idea. I think you should just stay here and talk to him."

"No, I don't want to talk to him. Not yet." The tears welled up in my eyes. "I can't yet, Jackie. It just hurts too much right now." I sniffed and fought to stop the tears.

"Come with us. You can help me. You're strong and will be able to help me."

"I have to work. I can't leave."

"Well, please do me a favor. Whatever you do, no matter how much he begs, please, please, please, don't tell him where I am."

"I won't. I need to go home, but call me and tell me what you find for flights. I need to make sure you're okay."

"The only way to make sure I'm fine is to come with me."

"Yeah." Jackie stood and looked at me. I stood to walk her out. When we reached the door, she wrapped me in an embrace. "Nikki, please don't do anything crazy, and make sure to call me."

"I promise, I will." I pulled back and looked her in the eyes. "I just can't bear the thought of facing him, or losing him. I can't even begin to imagine living without him. I love him so much." I choked out through my tears.

"I know." Jackie rubbed down my hair, down my arm, then left.

I went to retrieve my laptop. I sat at the breakfast bar and began my flight search. I picked up the phone and called Sky. I left him a voicemail asking if he could keep Abby until Wednesday evening. If he could keep her, I just needed to know. I'd found low-priced flights for Jessica, Alexander, and myself. If he couldn't, I'd need to get her on the flight with us and he'd have to get her on another weekend.

It took him a few minutes to return my call. He was going to keep Abby. He kept asking me what was going on, but I couldn't involve him. I had shared far more information with him than I should have. I was learning, keep Sky out of our relationship. I thanked him for his concern, but assured him I would be fine. The words came out of my mouth, but I wasn't positive I was speaking the truth.

When I hung up the call with him, Jackie called me.

"Hey, Jackie."

"Okay."

"Okay what?"

"Okay, I'm going to go with you. I kind of stretched the truth to my job and told them I had a family emergency and had to be out of town until Thursday."

"Thank you. Please don't tell a soul where we're going. I don't want him to know. By the time I get back, I'll be ready to deal with him."

****

We landed and took a cab to our hotel. We were in a hotel just off the strip and I had booked two adjoining rooms.

The hope that I would feel better once I got away was short-lived. I didn't feel better. I felt terrible. I felt like I was running from the inevitable. But even more so, my heart broke for Jeff. I shouldn't have given a damn about his feelings, but I did.

He was going to come home to an empty house and have only a note from me. I was gone, and his son was gone. A part of me wanted to feel him in my arms. I wanted him to tell me none of what Jason had said was true.

There were too many unresolved feelings and thoughts. Maybe in a couple days things would make more sense. Hopefully.

Having Alexander with me helped to keep me focused, but looking at his face made me think about Jeff. Jessica was filled in on everything as she listened to Jackie and me talk. She didn't offer her opinion. I could see in her eyes that she felt like she was caught in the middle of a bad situation. But she really wasn't. She didn't have to pick sides or decide who was right or wrong. All I wanted her to do was listen, and help me with Alexander if I needed a break. I certainly couldn't leave her in our house while I was gone. I was already wondering if Jeff was having sex with that wretched Blake. The thought of that made me sick and brought so many bad thoughts into my mind.

A couple days after we had been in Las Vegas, Jackie and I were lying poolside at the resort. Jessica had stayed in the room with Alexander. It was far too hot for him, and she wasn't fond of the excessive heat either.

Jackie tapped at my arm. "Listen to this song. This is Me'Shell Ndegeocello."

The music coming through the iPod summed up exactly how I felt and exacerbated my pain. *You made a fool of me, tell me why.*

A tear slid from my closed eyes as I laid back in the lounge chair.

"I'm going to get a drink. Do you want anything, Nikki?"

"Just a water, please," I choked out. I wiped the tears from my face as I watched her slip on her flip-flops.

"Sure thing. I'll be right back."

Jackie stood up and faced the pool bar over near the entrance to the hotel and gasped.

She stopped dead in her tracks.

"Why are you just standing there? Are you okay?" I was dying of thirst and really wanted that bottle of water.

"You've got to be shitting me," she muttered. "Nikki ..."

End of Book 2

About the Author

Desiree was born and raised in Iowa. She married her high school sweetheart and moved to the Philadelphia area after high school and has been happily married for over twenty-five years. She's the mother of two sons and a daughter.

Writing has always been a part of her life. It started as a way to cope with her childhood shyness, allowing her to communicate without talking. Now she talks and writes ... and talks. Desiree also enjoys traveling and spending time at the beach.

Over the past two plus years, she's been working to get her thoughts in print. She is finally writing what she wants to write. *Twisted by Desire* is her debut novel.

A Note from Desiree

Thank you for reading my book. I hope you enjoyed reading it as much as I enjoyed writing it. I'm honored and humbled that you chose to continue reading Nikki and Jeff's story.

If you did enjoy the book, I'd be forever grateful if you'd be kind enough to leave a review on Amazon and Goodreads for me.

If you'd like to send me direct feedback, please email me at desirecox69@gmail.com or PM me on Facebook. I'd love to hear from you and will respond to each email I receive.

You can also connect and communicate with me through my other social media sites:

Facebook -
https://www.facebook.com/DesireeACoxAuthor?ref=hl

Amazon Author Page -
http://www.amazon.com/Desiree-A.-Cox/e/B00QODW54G/ref=sr_ntt_srch_lnk_1?qid=1426635913&sr=8-1

Goodreads -
https://www.goodreads.com/author/show/8326258.Desiree_A_Cox

Twitter -

https://twitter.com/DesireeACox

Pinterest -

http://www.pinterest.com/desireecox564/

Google+ -

https://plus.google.com/115253355587352296635/posts?hl=en

Next Up

My short story, *Fantasy Come True,* is part of the Wickedly Exotic Spring Erotic Wonderland Box Set – Available now on Amazon and Smashwords.

Look for *Reclaimed By Desire*, Book 3 in the Lust, Desire and Love Trilogy - Summer 2015.